MW01139152

From the Agatha and Macavity Award-Nominated Author of
Full Mortality

RACING FROM EVIL
A Nikki Latrelle Mystery Novella
The Prequel

Sasscer Hill
Wildspirit Press, 2016

Cover Art by Teresa, <u>DESIGNS BY BMB</u>

PRAISE FOR THE NIKKI LATRELLE MYSTERY SERIES

"Sasscer, the honor comes in your accomplishments and talent, and you should take great pride in such a magnificent trifecta. Congratulations!!! Well done. Dick Francis lives!"

– Steve Haskin, Senior Correspondent, *Blood-Horse*. Former National Correspondent, *Daily Racing Form*, winner of eighteen awards for excellence in turf writing.

"This twisty and fast-paced page turner is cleverly plotted and genuinely entertaining—Hill's insider knowledge and love of the horse-racing world shines through on every page. Sasscer knows her stuff!"

- Hank Phillippi Ryan. Agatha, Anthony, Mary Higgins Clark, and Macavity Award–winning author

"If you miss the late Dick Francis's racetrack thrillers, you'll be intrigued by Sasscer Hill's Racing From Death"

– *The Washington Post*, August 29, 2012

"Hill, herself a Maryland horse breeder, is a genuine find, writing smooth and vivid descriptive prose about racetrack characters and backstretch ambience that reeks authenticity."

– John L. Breen, *Ellery Queen's Mystery Magazine*

"Sasscer Hill brings us another exciting racehorse mystery . . . an utterly unique take on racetrack thrillers." - Betty Webb, *Mystery Scene Magazine*, Summer Issue, 2012

"New novel about a Laurel Park jockey is a wild ride. While compared to Dick Francis and Sue Grafton, Hill's work reflects her respect for horse racing and the influence of the late Walter Farley. A page-turner, the book's sentences are short and crisp. The action comes off as authentic."

- Sandra McKee, *Baltimore Sun*, April, 2012

"If you like the work of Dick Francis or Sue Grafton, you will like Sasscer Hill. With a true insider's knowledge of horse racing, Hill brings us Nikki Latrelle, a young jockey placed in harm's way who finds the courage to fight the odds and the heart to race for her dreams."

–Mike Batttaglia, NBC racing analyst and TV host.

"This is a major new talent and the comparisons to Dick Francis are not hyperbole."

—Margaret Maron, New York Times Best selling author and winner of the Edgar, Agatha, Anthony, and Macavity awards.

"Facing potential death and long hidden secrets in her family, 'Racing from Death' is an exciting thriller set in the world of horse racing, very much recommended."

– Carl Logan, *Midwest Book Review*, February 8, 2013

"Nikki is one of the most appealing fictional characters I've ever met. You are rooting for her every inch of the way. The descriptions of backstretch life are enchanting."

– Lucy Acton, Editor of *Mid-Atlantic Thoroughbred*

"I thoroughly enjoyed *Full Mortality*–the pages fly by, the characters are vivid, and Hill captures life on the backstretch perfectly."

–Charlsie Cantey, racing analyst for ESPN, ABC, CBS and NBC.

"Anyone reading *The Sea Horse Trade*, needs to be sure to have plenty of time because it's impossible to put it down."

– Martha Barbone, *Horse of Delaware Valley*, June 2013

This novella is dedicated to Sisters in Crime

ACKNOWLEDGEMENTS

A huge thanks to the individuals who took their time to answer medical questions about drugs and technical questions about racing procedure.

Judy Melinek, M.D., PathologyExpert, Inc., and
Denver Beckner, Maryland Jockey Club.

1

My name is Nikki Latrelle, and people tell me my childhood was a nightmare. That isn't true. Maybe I was fatherless, and Mom and I didn't have much, but it was okay until she brought Stanley Rackmeyer into our home. That's when the bad stuff began.

Before that, we had some good times. When I was nine, Mom took me for my first visit to Pimlico racetrack. I was horse crazy and filled with an excitement that seemed to razz Mom as much as it did me.

After rushing through the cavernous interior of the grandstand, we crossed the concrete apron outside, and pushed against the track railing. The third race was about to go off, and the post parade was approaching.

Leading the field was a dark bay with a white blaze. I'd never seen a Thoroughbred racehorse before. I'd never seen anything so beautiful.

His neck was bowed, he was on his toes, and his eyes were partially hidden by blinkers. As he came past me, he turned his head, revealing a bright, liquid eye that stared right at me. He pricked his ears, ducked his head in my direction, and nickered.

The sound pierced my heart.

My mom, Helen Latrelle, loved horses too, and she liked to bet a little. Being at the track with her was always fun. She seemed more carefree and relaxed there. After that first day, she took me to Pimlico quite often during live racing. When the action moved over to Laurel Park racetrack in the winter, we'd take a bus out the Baltimore Washington Parkway, and watch the ponies run at Laurel.

All those times we went to the track only one bad thing ever happened. It was the day Mom gave me a five-dollar bill to buy hot dogs and sodas while she sat on a bench with her red pen and handicapped the next race.

I had the five clutched in my hand, when an older boy with white blond hair, eyebrows, and lashes swung toward me and began to walk alongside as I headed for the grill. It was on the far side of a supporting wall that divided sections of the grandstand, and as I walked past the cinder block partition, he shoved me into the wall, knocking me to the concrete floor. He snatched the bill, and turned to run.

"Hey," I yelled, "that's mine!"

He stared at me with irises almost as dark as his pupils, making his eyes appear like black holes in his pale skin. His expressionless eyes and ghost-white face frightened me, and my outrage dwindled into tears. I ran back to Mom as fast as my young legs would carry me, sobbing.

Fortunately, I never saw him again. At least, not when I went with Mom to the track.

Though I shared Mom's blue eyes and brown hair, I always thought she was prettier. She had big, warm eyes, and her mouth was full. Sometimes I'd notice men looking at her.

I don't remember my dad. A heart attack took him when I was two years old. His father's family, who lived somewhere in Iowa, was indifferent to us, and my mother had no use for them. Like me, Mom was an only child, and when I was five, her parents died in a plane crash. From then on, we were on our own.

My mom managed to land a job as a cook at Miss Potter's School for Girls. The school was what Mom called "exclusive," with a bunch of rich girls from "nice" families. It even had stables and offered riding lessons to its wealthy students.

Mom would take the city bus up 83 at seven each morning, and get off north of the Baltimore Beltway. The area near the school was studded with expensive homes, so unlike our narrow row house with its barred windows and leaky roof.

I had a key, and after school, I'd walk home and let myself into the dark, narrow house on a street off Garrison Avenue. Crammed between two other row houses with windows only at the front and rear, we didn't get much light.

As a ten-year-old, I was thrilled when Mom told me she'd finagled the school into giving me riding lessons on Saturdays in exchange for my help with stable chores. She took me to a shop that sold used equestrian clothing and bought me a pair of rubber riding boots, a helmet, and britches.

The following weekend, we took a bus north and arrived at the school early, before the riding classes began. It was a sunny morning in fall, but the air held a chill, as if warning about the winter to come.

We walked past the fancy stone buildings of Potters' campus and into the barn, where I breathed in the smell of horses, and the mingled scents of hay, grain, molasses and manure. Somewhere inside a stall, a horse nickered and a bucket rattled. A calico barn cat hopped off a bale of hay and rubbed herself against my leg. I leaned down to pet her.

"So this is Nikki?"

Startled, I straightened and saw a tall, weather-beaten woman with a slight limp emerging from the shadows farther back in the barn. She wore an old wool jacket, and a frayed tweed cap. Her hair was steel gray, her hands wrinkled. When she reached me, she gazed down with an unreadable expression.

Mom nodded at me encouragingly. "Answer Miss Boyle, Nikki. She'll be your instructor."

I stared at the floor and dragged the toe of one boot through the dirt leaving a wavy line. "Um, yeah. I'm Nikki."

"Come on, let's get your pony out and see what you can do." Her voice was gravely, which I would soon learn was from yelling at her students for so long. Behind her back, they called her "Boiler."

She brought out a dappled gray pony, tacked him up, and boosted me into the saddle. The pony shifted his weight and tossed his head. As he moved beneath me he snorted, and the resulting vibration coursed through my body. Something stirred deep inside me. I felt like I'd come home.

Leading the pony into a nearby ring, Miss Boyle put the reins in my hands, and stepped away.

"Okay," she said, "walk him around the ring."

I'd watched westerns on TV, but had no real idea what I was supposed to do. Some instinct must have kicked in. I picked up the reins, thumped the pony gently with my heels, and clucked. He stepped forward and we moved sedately around the enclosure.

Miss Boyle gave my mother a funny look. "Helen, I thought you said the girl has never ridden."

"She hasn't."

"Then she's a natural."

It didn't take me long to realize I was a charity case, and that the Bitsies, Muffies, and Bumpsies at the school knew it. The first time I rode in the beginner's class with other students, the real lesson I learned was that money separates people. Dressed in my new-to-me clothes, I was surrounded by girls wearing fine leather boots and beautiful tweed riding coats with velvet collars.

As the school horses plodded around the dirt ring, I listened to the girls' chatter. Their speech was polished and clipped. They talked about things I'd never heard of like martingales, finger bowls, and skiing in Vale.

I caught them stealing glances at me like I was an oddity, and some of the glances said an oddity that didn't belong.

As the horses circled the enclosure, I couldn't help staring at a deep teal jacket, the color rich against a black velvet collar.

When its owner caught me looking, she said, "You like my coat? Mummy bought it for me in London. You'd probably like my blue one even more."

"You're not in school here, are you?" a girl named Bitsi asked, swiveling her upper body to stare back at me as I rode behind her. She had shiny, curly blond hair tied with a black ribbon.

"No," I said, gazing at my hands gripping the reins. "I'm just taking lessons."

She continued to stare, "But who *are* you?"

She made me nervous. I tried but couldn't find the words to answer her.

"She's the cook's daughter," the girl riding behind me said. "I can't *imagine* why she's here."

In the middle of the ring, living up to her nickname, "Boiler" slapped her riding crop hard against her boot. Her mouth twisted with annoyance.

"Pay attention to what you're doing Muffy. Your horse is about to walk into the back of Nikki's pony. Your reins are sloppy. And you need to get your heels down!"

I stared straight ahead through my pony's ears, afraid to look at anyone. Focusing on the warm animal beneath me, I patted his chestnut neck. The strength of his muscles and the silky feel of his hair soothed me, easing a little of the hurt inflicted by the other girls.

At my public school the next week, I made myself feel better by mimicking Muffy's prissy accent and behavior to amuse my classmates. Every week, I had a new "Miss Pompous" story to tell my school chums Letitia, and Carmen. My descriptions would leave them giggling and making rude noises. After a while, I could copy those prissy Potter voices and affected mannerisms perfectly.

Six months later, amid baleful looks and snide comments about "teacher's pet," I was promoted to the intermediate riding class, where the young women seemed more interested in riding than in picking on me. Still, I was an outsider, and an invisible wall rose between us.

At the end of that first year, Boiler surprised me, asking me to stay on during summer riding camp. There was no school during those months and Mom wouldn't be working in the kitchen. I'll never know what favors Boiler called in to make this happen, but her kindness meant I could ride five days a week. For me, it was like winning a trip to Disney World.

Riding camp chiseled a bit at that invisible wall. Everyone had to groom the horses, bed down the stalls, and clean the tack. It made us more of a team and brought some of those girls down a peg or two.

Out of all the students, Jill, was one of the few who treated me with kindness. She had brown hair she wore in pigtails and braces on her teeth. A constellation of freckles spread across her nose beneath eyes that were filled with confidence. She didn't seem to care what others thought.

"Do you like to read?" she asked me. We were cleaning bridles, and the smell of saddle soap and horse sweat hung strong in the air around us.

"I guess," I said. Mom wasn't a reader, and had never encouraged me. We had no books at home, anyway. "I don't really read that much."

"You don't *read?*" Her eyes widened as if she couldn't imagine such a thing.

Embarrassed, I shook my head and shrugged.

"But you *can* read, right?"

"Of course I can!"

The anger in my voice didn't faze her. "Good. Then, I'll bring you some books tomorrow."

The next day, after classes and chores, she handed me a canvas bag filled with books by Walter Farley. "Read 'The Black Stallion' first. You'll love it."

What if I didn't? What if I hated it? Should I pretend I liked it? But when I opened the book at home, and met the Black on page six—"beautiful, savage, splendid"—the same emotional response welled up inside me that I'd felt for that first racehorse at Pimlico.

I couldn't put the books down, and when I finished them, Jill gave me more. During the next two years, she lent me books from the school's summer reading lists, from the classics to the latest novels from pop culture.

Vivid, well-told fiction novels taught me that people have been acting out the same stories forever. They love, they are kind, sometimes heroic, and often as not, they betray, cheat and con one another. And sometimes they lie, even to themselves.

The day I realized my mother was lying, I was spun into a terrible place. A place where I had to grow up fast.

2

By the time I turned twelve, my days at Potters had become the best ones of my life.

One Saturday, when I was doing my after class chores, I saw a van pull in outside the barn. Next, I heard hooves stomping on a ramp, as apparently, a horse was unloaded on the van's far side.

Boiler hurried into the barn from her office. "Nikki, stop what you're doing and come look at this horse. His name is Wishful."

I jogged around the back of the van and studied the new horse. A chestnut gelding with a white blaze and four white stockings, he stood on the end of a lead line held by the man from the shipping company. Boiler took the horse and led him into the barn.

"What do you think, Nikki?"

I continued to inspect the horse, liking him, not sure how much to say.

"Speak up," Boiler said, "I'm not going to stand here all day."

"He's younger, thinner and a lot more fit than our other horses."

"What else?"

"He looks intelligent and ... proud."

"That's my girl. Get that Stuben saddle you like and see if it fits him. I'll get a bridle. I'm thinking a snaffle bit will work."

Darned if she wasn't as excited as I was. We got him ready, took him to the ring, and I climbed aboard. Just before I settled in the saddle, Wishful tried to scoot out from under me, but Boiler kept a firm hold on his rein until I got settled.

As she'd done that first day, she let go, and said, "Okay, walk him around."

Our turn about the ring went smoothly at the walk and trot. Boiler's scrutiny was intense.

"Okay, ask him to canter."

I did, and he busted forward, quickly gaining speed until I got my feet on the dashboard and pulled him up. I felt giddy.

"You look like you just won the lottery," she said. "What do you think of him now?"

"He has a really light mouth, his walk is powerful and very forward, his trot's wonderful, and he's fast as shi–uh, really fast."

"I want you to teach him to jump."

"*Me?*"

"Nikki, don't be coy. You know you're the best rider here." She gave me her hard look. "But if you tell anyone I said that, I'll call you a liar!"

I flinched, making Wishful tense beneath me, until the tiny smile at the corners of Boiler's mouth gave her away.

"My lips are sealed," I said.

She nodded. "You've been jumping well, and your hands and seat are just what Wishful needs. The school bought this horse so the team could win some shows next spring. I want you to go on with him."

Her faith in me was wonderful, validating, but a little frightening. It was more pressure than I'd experience before, but most of all, it told me how far I'd come in two years, how lucky I was, and what a wonderful thing Mom had done for me.

"I'm going to lay a few poles on the ground. You walk him over and see what he thinks about it."

I did, he liked it, and a month later, I had him going over a course of one to two feet. He was a natural jumper, nimble around tight corners, with plenty of speed. The two of us had a future.

As the days darkened into winter, the weather turned cold and wet. Our leaky roof, now over thirty years old, continued to deteriorate. It got so bad, Mom set out buckets in both of the upstairs bedrooms to collect the rainwater. The ceilings darkened with wet stains. The roof had been patched too many times, and we desperately needed a new one. But there wasn't enough money.

The morning Mom said she was having a guy come look at the roof, I was curious. Being older, I'd figured out the pile of papers she hid in a folder were bills. Unpaid bills, the worst being our mortgage, and something she finally told me was called a balloon payment.

"Mom, how can we afford to fix the roof?"

"I met a guy." That was all she said.

That Friday was a school holiday. Boiler raised the poles on the fences, and Wishful and I had a couple of glorious rounds of jumping. Then she lowered the poles a bit and brought out a stopwatch.

"If you win a class, and there's a jump-off, you're going to have to go for speed. Can you do that?"

I nodded, picked up the reins and eased Wishful into a trot. When I sat deeper in the saddle and pushed him with my legs and seat, he took off like a rocket. I had to collect him real quick to get him into each jump right, and then make sure I gave him his head as he lifted in the air for each jump. Each time we rose over the poles, I'd be looking for the next obstacle. Wishful and I were so connected he sensed what was coming next and went for it.

When we finished, I was laughing and Boiler's eyes seemed unusually bright.

"Nikki, you're a speed demon!"

Wishful was blowing and full of himself, and I couldn't stop grinning.

When I got home, Mom called me from the kitchen in the back of the house. "I'm in here, honey."

She was sitting at the metal table with its red-and-white checkered cloth. I stopped abruptly in the doorway. A man sat at the table with her. He was thin and hard looking, with a sharp face. His forehead, nose, and chin thrust out like the blade of a hatchet. I didn't like how comfortable he seemed in our kitchen. He must have brought the six-pack of beer on the table. He appeared to be into his second, and Mom had just emptied one of her own. The thing was, she almost never drank.

"Nikki, this is Stanley."

"Nice to meet ya," he said, his eyes studying me. He smelled like tar and had brown stains on his pant's legs.

I disliked him immediately and switched my gaze to the kitchen window where rain that had started on my way home ran in wavy rivulets down the glass. I could still feel his stare on me. I hated it.

"Stanley's a roofer," Mom said. "A&A Roofing. It's a good company, and he's going to put on a new one for us!"

But why was he in our kitchen drinking beer? And why was Mom in that tight blouse, and wearing so much perfume?

That night, I lay in bed listening to the steady splash of water drops in the bucket near my bed. I felt out of sorts, like I saw things differently. What used to be familiar wasn't anymore.

As the water beaded on the ceiling overhead, I began to think about my mother, Helen, in ways I hadn't considered before. Was she lonely? Did she like this man Stanley? He was tough looking and wiry. Was she attracted to him? Did she want him to be . . . her *boyfriend*? The thought made me cringe. I couldn't stand him. His eyes and voice were too friendly when he looked at Mom, and I didn't like it.

During breakfast the next morning, I tried to speak to her, but the words wouldn't come. Mom started chewing on her lower lip and avoiding my eyes. Finally, she met my gaze.

"What is it, Nikki?"

"Does Mr. Rackmeyer have to come inside our house when he does the roof?"

"Why would you ask that? Stanley's a nice guy. We're *lucky* I met him. He's giving us a big break on the cost of the roof."

"Why?"

My question made her lips compress. "I *told* you. He's a nice guy. I don't want to hear any more about this from you. We need his help. Do you like listening to water drip in your room all night? I sure don't!"

Two days later, Mom went out after dinner and didn't get home until late. I could smell the perfume and beer on her. I could smell tar and some other scent I didn't recognize and didn't like. A few days after that, when she came home from her job, Stanley was with her.

He gave me a smile like a rodent baring its teeth. "How ya doin' kid?"

"Okay."

"She don't say much, does she Helen?"

"She's a good kid. Just a little shy sometimes."

"Yeah, whatever." He moved toward our staircase. "I wanna see those leaks upstairs." Without asking he went up like it was his own house. We followed.

I hated seeing him inside my bedroom. My skin crawled when he sat on the edge of my bed, picked up the stuffed horse I'd had for years and grinned as he stroked it.

"Nice horsey, Nikki."

When we went downstairs, Mom and Stanley had a beer in the kitchen. And when I asked Mom about dinner, Stanley said, "I'm taking you girls out tonight."

Mom blushed. "You don't need to do that, Stanley."

"Pretty girls like you two deserve it. It's settled." He took a big swallow of his beer. "This is a nice house ya got here, Helen. Solid brick. Foundation's sound. I get this roof fixed up, you'll be sitting pretty."

When they finished their beer, he took us to MacDonald's in his Chevy truck. It had a rack on top loaded with aluminum ladders that rattled and banged every time we hit a bump. The truck's cab was dirty, and smelled like burnt tar.

At McDonald's it was embarrassing how thrilled Mom was to have a man buy us dinner. Then I felt guilty for feeling that way.

When Stanley took us home, he parked his truck on the street, and came inside.

"I got homework," I said, and hurried upstairs to my room. But I stood in my doorway listening. I heard the tops on two beer cans pop, and the murmur of their voices, the words indecipherable until Stanley voice got louder and whiny.

"Come on baby, let me stay tonight. You know you want me to."

I thought I heard Mom say something about me, then he said, "She's gonna have to get used to it."

Mom's voice sounded uneasy as it reached me where I stood frozen in my doorway. I thought she said something like . . . "married first."

Stanley left soon after that and I prayed Mom had come to her senses and pushed Stanley out of our lives. But two days later, she came home with a ring on her finger and a happy glow on her face.

"Stanley and I are getting married." She looked at me, and I could tell she didn't like my obvious disappointment. "Listen, Nikki, we won't have to worry about that balloon payment anymore!"

When I didn't respond, she jerked her hands wide apart. "Can't you be happy for me?"

I stared at the kitchen's green linoleum floor and didn't answer.

3

They got married in the Baltimore City Courthouse on a Wednesday. I begged off and went to school instead, where my math teacher snapped at me for not paying attention and "being in another world."

That evening, Stanley took us to Applebee's to celebrate, except I had no appetite and could hardly swallow my food.

Across the table, the eyes in that hatchet face stared at me, the lips flattened in annoyance. "What's the matter with you, kid? You upset about something?"

"I'm just tired."

"Maybe you shouldn't ride so much. What do you think Helen? She need to ride all the time?"

"She really likes it, Stan. It's good for her."

"If you say so. Me, I ain't so sure."

After that I tried to hide my feelings. I'm surprised my face didn't crack from my pasted-on smile.

If it hadn't been for Boiler, Jill, and Wishful, I don't know how I would have made it through the following spring, summer, and fall. Boiler talked the school's headmistress into letting me ride on the team that spring, and Wishful and I cleaned up, winning many of the individual classes in shows with rival schools. The Potter's team went on to the championships, and the walls of my bedroom were lined with blue ribbons. But most important, the horses kept me sane.

Stanley, true to his word, put a new roof on the house with a couple of his crew, and they patched and painted the bedroom ceilings. It was all Mom talked about.

"Nikki, hasn't Stan been wonderful? We're so snug and safe now!"

"Whatever."

"Nikki, I hate that word. Please *answer* me."

"Mr. Rackmeyer is wonderful, okay?"

She shook her head, her lips a thin line.

By that time Stanley had taken over the couch in our living room where he watched sports on TV and drank beer every night. I stayed in my bedroom with my books. The stories opened another world and a temporary escape from Stanley.

But even the best novel couldn't blot out the noises that came from Mom and Stanley's room late at night. They made me sick, and most nights I ended up with the clock radio jammed against my ear.

But Mom seemed happy. She had new clothes, and Stanley bought them a fancy king-sized bed. So I sucked it up, or at least tried to, until I neared my thirteenth birthday. By then, I'd changed enough, that for months, Stanley had been looking at me differently, and one night when I came downstairs for a soda, my life took an ugly turn.

He was on the couch with Mom watching a Ravens game. I could feel his eyes following me as I went by. When I walked back through with my drink, he whistled.

"Helen, look at our girl. She's sprouting tits. Gonna be a real looker, like you."

Mom's lips compressed. "Don't talk like that, Stan. You're making her uncomfortable."

"Damn, woman. I'll talk how I wanna talk. She's gonna have guys beating our door down, so she might as well get used to it."

Mom stiffened, and he put an arm around her. "Relax, honey, I didn't mean nothing."

After that I wore baggy tops and spent as much time as possible in my room or at Carmen or Letitia's house. After they met Stanley, they didn't come over to our house anymore, and that fall, I was glad when it got cold, providing an excuse to hide myself under even more layers. I figured if I was careful, he'd leave me alone.

Near Christmas, Mom made eggnog. But Stanley said it was too weak and made a run to the corner liquor store for a bottle of Jack Daniels. When he got home, he went out to the wood porch in the back of the house. It was freezing out there, and where Mom liked to use it to store her bucket of eggnog. Stanley poured the whole bottle of bourbon into the mixture.

Mom and I stood in the kitchen doorway watching him, listening to the gurgle of booze coming out of the bottle.

"Jesus, Stanley. You're going to knock us out," she said. But then she giggled. She'd already had a glass of the weaker version, which had plenty of bourbon and rum.

I was ready to bolt for my room, but Stanley said, "Hey, sweetie, don't leave. You're always runnin' off to your room. Sit with us and have a glass. It's Christmas, for Christ's sake."

He got three glasses and ladled them half full. I looked at Mom. She shrugged, gave me a weak smile. "Go on, you're old enough for a sip or two."

"Come on, girls." He led us to the kitchen table, Mom lit the red Christmas candle in the center, and we sat.

They drank up. I sniffed the concoction and took a sip. If it hadn't been loaded with cream, sugar, and nutmeg, I would have spit it out. I swallowed, and felt it burn all the way down.

Stanley kept glancing at me as he drank. Mom seemed oblivious.

"Nikki," she said, "now that your ceiling's fixed, I was thinking about getting new curtains for your bedroom. Would you like that?"

"Uh, sure." I pushed my glass away, "I don't think I want any more of this stuff."

Stanley pushed up from his chair. "Babe, you are wasting some really fine shit." He moved around the table to where I sat. "I'll drink it for you." He leaned over, brushing his hand across one of my breasts as he reached for my glass.

Mom saw him do it, but she looked away, and said nothing.

That's when I knew she was a liar.

Four weeks later on a bitter cold January day, I was called out of history class to the principal's office. I had no idea why, but I rubbed my arms as an inner chill hit me in the long tiled hallway.

Mr. Wheatley, or "Wheaties," as the students called him, waved me into his office, his face and eyes tight with some emotion. He gestured at the metal chair before his desk

"Nikki, please sit down."

I did, and he got right to it.

"I'm sorry to tell you. Your mother passed away this morning."

"No. That's not possible."

"You know how icy it is outside. She slipped from the curb. A city bus was coming. I'm so sorry." He took a short breath. "It happened fast. They say she probably didn't feel any pain."

"No!" I felt like I was splitting in half. "She can't be gone."

"I'm so sorry," he said again.

I tried to digest what had happened. What this meant. A rush of fear hit me. I wrapped my arms around my sides.

"I understand how hard this must–"

"You don't. I can't . . . I won't live with my stepfather!"

He looked startled, and then seemed to give my outburst some thought. "If there is a problem with your stepfather, we can have Social Services step in."

I stared at him. "I don't want Social Services."

"The difficulty, Nikki, is your file doesn't show any direct family. You don't have a grandparent, aunt, or uncle?"

"No. There's no one." My hands started shaking and I felt nauseous.

Over the next three days the house was filled with people. Mom's two friend's from Potter's kitchen staff brought pans of lasagna and meatloaf, while neighbors brought flowers and more dishes of food. I was grateful when Carmen and Letitia came with their mothers.

But Boiler didn't come. Her absence gave me a lost feeling. She had to know. Maybe she'd be at the funeral.

With all the people coming and going, Stanley left me alone except for the afternoon he asked to see my cell phone.

"Want kind of phone you got there, Nikki?"

"Just an Android."

"Lemme see it. Come on, hand it to me."

When I did, he put it in the pocket of his work vest. "We can't afford for you to have this, kid. We gotta watch the money now that Helen's salary's gone."

"But I *need* that," I said.

"Maybe later. If you're a good girl." He had a triumphant little smile as he turned to walk away from me.

From then on, I locked my door every night, even pushing my armchair against it. I never cried. Instead, I'd lie in bed, fully clothed, staring blindly at the new ceiling, while my thoughts scrabbled around my head like rats in a cage.

On the fourth day there was a simple memorial service. Stanley had arranged for it at the nearest funeral parlor. There was no church, no burial. He had my mother cremated and told the funeral parlor to get rid of the ashes.

Again, my disappointment and confusion were sharp when Boiler didn't come.

About ten people showed up at the house afterwards and when they left, I knew they wouldn't be back. Not after hearing Carmen's mother whispering to our neighbor Mrs. Gonzales as they sat on the couch. They didn't realize I was standing behind them.

Carmen's mother whispered so low I barely heard her. "Why did she marry him? He's just *awful*."

When Mrs. Gonzales answered, her voice sounded so contemptuous. "To get a new roof? Or maybe he's good in bed."

"Don't talk about my mother like that!"

Startled, they whipped their heads around to stare at me.

"Oh, Nikki," Mrs. Gonzales said. "I was just–"

"I hate you!" I bolted from the room and ran upstairs. Even then I didn't cry. Crying could keep me from being alert and on guard. I wasn't a kid anymore. I was *thirteen*. I should be able to figure out what to do.

My thoughts and their little rat feet scurried through my head, finally stopping someplace useful. *Boiler*. Maybe she would help me. I'd go to her in the morning.

But late that night, Stanley came to my room.

4

Sometime after midnight, the sound of footsteps awakened me. Stanley was outside my door. I'd known he would come. *Why hadn't I run?*

Something smashed against my door, low, near the floor. Stanley's steel-toed boot? Another crash. I heard the lock give way and a splintering sound from the wood.

Think Nikki. Think!

I sat up fast, rolling away from the noise, out of my bed, onto the floor. I reached underneath for my rubber riding boots. Stanley jammed the door open a few inches. As he forced the door open wider, the legs of my armchair screeched against the wood floor. As usual, I was wearing my street clothes. I pulled on the boots and leapt to my feet.

He was in the room. The overhead light flicked on.

"Nikki, sweetie, why aren't you in bed?" He wore his underwear and heavy boots.

I couldn't speak. My legs trembled. My pulse pounded in my ears.

He smiled, baring his rodent teeth. "You shouldn't be locking your door on me. I want us to get along, honey. I'm your friend." His teeth gleamed white. "Let me show you."

He grabbed the armchair and shoved it against the broken door, blocking me in the room.

As his eyes stroked up and down my body, a flame of rage curled in my belly.

He circled the end of the bed, walking toward me. "Come on, sweetie. I won't hurt you."

I ran straight at him and kicked his privates as fast and hard as I could.

He doubled over with pain. "You *bitch!*"

I darted to the window, shoved it open enough to squeeze through, and rolled onto the fire escape. When I pushed on the ladder, the old hinge wouldn't release to let the ladder down. Stanley was at the window trying to raise it.

Oh, God. I threw my weight on the ladder, gasping with relief when the metal rungs dropped to the ground. I scurried to the bottom, fear and adrenalin giving me wings.

I hit the ground with a jolt, before sprinting through the backyard, and flinging myself over the metal fence. A nervous glance up at my window showed no sign of Stanley. I sped down the alley to the street out front, where I paused in the dark between two streetlights. The cold had seeped into my clothes until the fabric felt icy against my skin.

The front door flew open. Stanley, who'd thrown on a bathrobe, stood there, his eyes searching. I ran. My spare frame and rubber boots created little sound on the pavement. Terrified, I looked back. He still loomed in the doorway. Maybe he hadn't seen me.

I have no money. No phone.

Should I run to a neighbor? Try to reach the nearest police station? What if they took me back to Stanley? He could say I was reacting to the stress of Mom's death, and the best place for me was safe at home with him. I couldn't risk it.

As I ran down my dark street and turned onto Garrison, it came to me. The place I'd been happiest. With Mom. A place I'd felt safe, a place close enough to run to. A place I could hide.

Pimlico.

Gasping for air, I had to slow to a walk on Garrison. No one was on the street, and there were no lights inside the houses as people slept through the night. I couldn't run anymore, but it was so cold, I had to move. I started a slow jog, the motion warming me a little. If I kept moving, I'd be all right.

I hit Park Heights Avenue and hung a left. Two more blocks, and I made a right onto Belvedere. I was close. On my left was an expanse of empty, crumbling pavement, a parking area that filled with cars and buses when Pimlico held its big races. Just beyond, lay the dirt track and the turn where the horses rolled into the backstretch.

I kept going. The land ahead swept down to a triangle of backstretch stables lying between Belvedere Avenue, Pimlico Road and the track railing.

As I got closer, I saw razor wire crowning the chain link fence between me and the stables. *Screw it.* I started climbing, afraid I'd lose my momentum, afraid I'd collapse from cold, or fear.

When I was high enough to touch the barbed wire, I pulled off a rubber boot, slid my hand inside, and pushed the boot against the rusty barbs. It folded over the wire, and with one hand in the boot and the other pressed against the rubber, I managed to swing one leg over.

The muscles of my arms trembled from the effort of holding the trunk of my body over the wire now running between my outstretched legs. Pain shot down my arms. My shoulders burned. Pushing with what little strength remained, I got the other leg over, whimpering as my unprotected hand slipped and a cluster of barbs ripped my palm and fingers.

I had to let go. The ground flew up to meet me, hard and fast, knocking the air out of me. Jolted with pain, I lay still a moment, before carefully testing each limb. I found my boot next to me and pulled it on, thinking I was okay, knowing I was safer with the razor wire between me and Stanley. After rolling to my hands and knees, I stood up and it didn't hurt that badly.

Maybe nine or ten barns stretched into the distance, varying in length according to their position inside the backstretch triangle. The stables were dark, the only illumination coming from a few overhead security lights, the only sound from light traffic in the distance.

Looking up, I realized that one of the longest barns had rooms overhead, like the second story of a motel. There would be people there. I avoided it and found a barn where the big wooden sliding door had been left open wide enough for me to slip inside.

Warmer air immediately hit my face and hands. The spice of liniment and the sweet scent of molasses and hay rolled over me. Riding beneath were the pungent odors of manure and the ammonia produced by horse urine. The mixed brew smelled like Boiler's barn and was incredibly comforting. Still, it was cold. And dark.

I inched forward and nearby a horse snorted. Listening, I heard the sound of molars grinding hay, hooves shifting in the straw. Several horses rattled their feed tubs, probably hoping I'd come to feed them.

I heard a soft nicker, and as I slowly approached the sound in the darkness, my outstretched hands touched a velvety muzzle and felt warm breath blowing against my fingers. The horse generated an extraordinary amount of heat that I needed desperately.

Dropping my hands, my fingers touched a rubber stall guard and some rubber-covered chains that kept the horse inside. I squatted down, eased underneath and felt my way to a far corner of the stall, the horse turning and following me.

The corner was fluffed with dry, clean hay. I curled into a ball and pulled as much fodder as I could over my body. The horse stood over me, his head just above my shoulder. He lowered his muzzle and sniffed at my hair, his soft rubberlike lips gently moving across my scalp.

Something broke loose inside me. Long held tears burned my eyes, and I wept with deep, gulping sobs. For Mom, for myself, for the fear, anger, and loneliness that overwhelmed me.

5

I woke up often that night. Each time, the unknown horse stood over me, blowing soft breath on my cheek or nuzzling my hair with fingerlike lips. I'd reach for his velvet nose with my hand, the connection reassuring and allowing me to sink back into a light sleep.

The barn was still dark when my stall mate and the horses around us became restless. I sat up quickly, stiff with cold, sore muscles, and fear. The barn lights came on, and the horses whickered and stomped. I thought grooms must have arrived to feed, making the horses eager for breakfast.

With the light, I could see the horse that had stood guard over me through the night. He was a big gray gelding with a dark mane and tail and white anklets on his front legs. The nose I'd touched so often during the night had a pink mark that looked just like a rosebud. The horse was gorgeous, and I was honored he'd treated me so kindly.

I was startled by a noise in the barn aisle. A dark-skinned man with dreads leaned over the webbing of our stall and dumped a pail of sweet feed into the bucket clipped on the wall just inside.

When he spotted me, his brows rose. "Hey girl, what you doing back there?"

"Uh, I'm . . . I'm looking for a job."

He shook his head, smiling. "Not gonna find it in Silver Punch's hay. Boss in his office. Why don't you ask him?"

"Okay." I tried not to look as busted as I felt. "So this horse is called Silver Punch?"

"Never you mind. You'd better come outta there."

"Okay."

It's hard to act nonchalant when you're covered with hay, pieces of straw, and horse hair, but I gave it my best shot. I brushed myself off and ducked under the webbing. The man stepped back to give me room, then pointed.

"Office down there at the end."

As I walked in the direction he'd indicated, I could hear him muttering. "Looking for a job, my ass. Runaway's what she is."

I didn't want a job. I wanted food, warmth, and bus fare to reach Boiler at Potter's School.

As I hurried down the dirt aisle, a man in an olive-green jacket and wool cap emerged from the office, stopped, and stared at me, his head tilting to one side like a curious bird.

"You lost?"

"No sir. Uh, maybe a little."

"Maybe a little? Looks like you've been sleeping in one of my stalls. How'd you get in here?"

"Sorry. I'll leave right now."

But a smile started to build on his mouth. "You hungry?"

I nodded.

"Thought so." He put his hand in his pocket and pulled out a ten-dollar bill. "You cold?" When I nodded again, he said, "You can get breakfast at the kitchen a few barns over."

"Yes, sir."

"Wait a minute."

I paused, ready to bolt.

"Jesus, you're as wary as a barn cat. Take this." He pulled more bills from his coat. "After you eat, there's a used clothing store on Belevedere. Get yourself a coat or something. But, listen. You can't stay here."

"Yes, sir." I reached for the money, stepped back quickly, clutching the bills in my hand."

As I scurried away, I thought I heard him mutter something about a "feral cat."

The kitchen turned out to be a tiny restaurant with good food sold cheap. It was filled with track help, like the guy who'd fed Silver Punch, and a mixture of Latinos and whites. They all stared, but nobody bothered me.

I got a plate of ham, eggs, and fried potatoes. Everyone was drinking coffee. I had hot chocolate. I wolfed the food down, and on my way to the stable gate, found a ladies room where I used the facilities and washed my hands. The water stung the cuts from the wire, but they didn't look too bad, and I was grateful Mom had made me get a tetanus shot a year earlier.

I leaned over the sink, scrubbed my face, and stood up. In the mirror a dark-haired scarecrow stared back. After drying my face on paper towels, I pulled the remaining pieces of hay and straw from my hair and clothes, then found my way to the backstretch gate.

The used clothing store had a hooded down-jacket that fit me and a pair of gloves for $1.00 that still had a $9.95 price tag attached. I found my bus stop and a short time later, was heading north.

Stepping off the warm bus, I zipped up my jacket, pulled the hood over my head, and pushed my hands into the jacket's deep pockets, grateful to the man who'd given me the money. I didn't even know his name.

I went through the stone gate at Potter's School, skirting the main buildings before walking to the barn in the rear. Inside, I greeted Wishful and gave him one of the horse treats Boiler kept in the feed room. I leaned over to pet the calico cat who rubbed her face against my leg. Boiler wasn't in the barn, so I went to the office and found her sitting at her desk with a spring horseshow schedule spread out on the wood surface.

When she saw me, she drew back, as if my presence alarmed her. She rubbed at her throat, and then her glance dropped away from me to the floor.

"Nikki, I heard the terrible news. I'm so very sorry about your mother."

"Thank you, Miss. Boyle."

The office heater kicked on and warm air and particles of paper dust floated toward me. I stared at the office shelves that were filled with equestrian text books, magazines, and volumes on veterinary medicine.

The silence became awkward until Boiler finally spoke. "I wish there was something I could do for you, but . . ." She stared at a point beyond my shoulder. "I'm surprised to see you here this morning. How are you?"

How was I? Why wouldn't she look at me? I don't know what I'd expected, but it wasn't this. I didn't answer her.

Now, she studied the scarred wood surface of her desk. Suddenly she stood up.

"I'm sick about this. Nikki, the board has decided you can't continue the lessons now that your mother–"

"I can't come here anymore?"

"If I had anything to say about it, you certainly could. Those people on the board are idiots! You have so much talent and promise. You're so smart."

Her anger was real. Relief flooded me as I realized she still wanted me there.

Her hands had clenched into fists. "Damn everything!" She paused a moment, then said, "I'm sorry, Nikki. But you probably should go home."

I was shocked by the small-child wail that erupted from my throat. "I can't go home!"

She came quickly around the desk and put her hands on my shoulders. "What is it?"

"My stepfather. He tried to, to . . ." I couldn't say it.

Shocked, her mouth parted before her lips curled in disgust. "Oh, my God. He didn't–"

"*No!* I ran away."

"My God, where did you go?"

I told her, poured out everything. By the time I was finished, I was shaking, and Boiler's face was white with anxiety.

"Sit down, Nikki. I'm going to make us some hot tea."

She did, and after handing me a cup, she said, "You are going to stay here tonight. I'd take you home with me, but I live with my sister. She's not well and . . ."

"That's okay. It would be really nice if I could sleep here."

"That settles it. You stay here, and we'll figure something out." But uncertainty clouded her eyes.

I didn't want to get her fired, but was really grateful for a place to stay. At least for now.

I slept in a sleeping bag on the sofa that night, a warmer, more comfortable bed than the stall of the night before. I woke up early, made more tea and had one of the sandwiches Boiler had bought the previous afternoon. Before I was halfway through feeding the horses, Boiler showed up and we finished together.

"I'm glad you're here, Nikki. It's Manuel's day off and I can use the help."

We turned the horses out into their paddocks and started cleaning stalls. These chores were usually done by the time I arrived, and it had never occurred to me how hard Boiler worked.

By ten o'clock the stalls and tack were clean, and I helped get five horses ready for the beginner class that started at eleven. The class finished a little before noon, and Boiler and I led the horses back to the barn until the next class.

We were about to leave the barn, when Boiler stopped. "I wonder who this is?"

I glanced at the newcomer, and froze. He wore a leather jacket, overalls and the boots he'd used to kick my door open.

"Oh, God. That's him," I whispered.

"Let me handle this," Boiler said, pushing me behind her.

"Mr. Redecker, is it? I'm Jane Boyle, Nikki's instructor. What can I do for you?

"Nice to meet you," he said, smiling pleasantly. "I'm her father. I've come to get her. Been worried about her 'cause she's been upset about her mother and all. I need to take her home."

"You're not taking her anywhere."

"What are you talking about?" he asked.

"Mr. Redecker, I know what you did."

He scowled, all pretense of being nice evaporating. He stepped closer to her, crowding her with his hatchet face and sharp shoulders.

Boiler stood her ground. "Nikki is *not* your daughter."

"Look, lady, I don't know what lies she'd told you. The kid's skipping school. You want, I can get the police to pick her up." He waved a dismissive hand at Boiler. "Come on, Nikki, we're going."

The anger I'd felt the night before flared hot. I scooted around Boiler. "It's not *your* home. It's mine, and I want you to get out!"

He laughed. "You little bitch. You think it's your house? Your mother signed half over to me when we got married. She didn't leave no will, so the house is mine now." His lips curved into the same smile of triumph I'd seen when he took my phone. "You better be nice to me," he said and grabbed my arm, twisting it, so I cried out.

Boiler leaned to one side and grabbed the rake that was propped against the barn wall. She smacked Stanley's face with it, and he dropped my arm.

"Run, Nikki, run," she cried.

I did, right into the barn. I glanced back to see her whack him with the rake again, but he grabbed it, threw it on the ground, and started after me.

I scurried up the barn ladder to the hay loft like a wild monkey, ran to the far end and opened the loft door. There was a ladder on the outside wall, and I flew down that even faster.

Running behind the barn, I raced along the black iron fence to a gap beneath it where rain water had formed a little ditch.

After rolling under the fence, I stood up to see Stanley climbing down the barn ladder in the distance. A city bus was about to pass me on the street. I ran along the side of the bus and beat on the door. The driver stopped long enough for me to get in, and I paid, using the last of the money the man at the track had given me. Stanley stood at the iron fence shaking his fist at me.

The bus was heading south, toward Pimlico.

6

As the bus rumbled toward the city, I sat next to a heavyset woman with a shopping bag at her feet. Old city buildings rolled past us outside the window, and I thought about Boiler, wondering why I'd never considered her life before, and how hard she must work at her job.

Maybe when you get older, you start thinking about other people, not just yourself. I wasn't the only one with hopes and dreams. What was it like for her to live with and take care of a sick sister? It had never occurred to me she didn't have enough money.

But it seemed everything was about money. It was why Mom had taken up with Stanley. It was why the girls at Potter's school could snicker and whisper about me. It was why they had tweed coats with velvet collars, and I didn't.

And now, Stanley had taken my home, and Mom had left me nothing. The knowledge lit black coals inside me, and their angry flame burned hot. She'd left no will and essentially, had given me to Stanley. Though I missed her desperately, a part of me almost hated her.

"Baby girl, you chew on your lip any harder and it's gonna bleed." It was the woman sitting next to me.

"Sorry," I said.

"What? You got nothing to be sorry about. I'm just saying, if I had a pretty mouth like yours, I wouldn't be chewing on it so hard."

I focused on her for the first time. Dark skin creased around tired eyes. Her brown coat and pants were old, and her sneakers had a hole over one big toe.

"Can't be all that bad," she said.

"I guess it could be worse."

"Yes, ma'am," she said. "It can *always* be worse."

We rode in silence, and my thoughts spun around like the bus wheels that carried us down the road. I had to earn a living, except I didn't know how. I just had to figure it out.

The bus finally reached my stop on Park Heights Avenue. Outside, it was cold, but my jacket was warm as I walked the few blocks along the avenue to Pimlico. The track was open for simulcast betting, but I had no money left to buy my way in.

When the ticket seller wasn't looking, I squatted low and scuttled under the turnstile like a crab. A couple of people saw me, but nobody said anything.

Nikki Latrelle, budding criminal.

Inside, the cement floor of the grandstand was only about a quarter filled with people. I figured they must be the hardcore bettors. Mostly older men, they studied *Daily Racing Forms*, drank beer from plastic cups and argued about their picks.

Near me, a man pointed a finger at a page he'd folded open on his *Form*. "Lenny you're nuts if you bet that horse! Last time, they passed the sumbitch like he was tied to the rail!"

Lenny shook his head in disagreement. "Yeah, well your rider is a fucking idiot."

The first man put his hand on his friend's shoulder and nodded in my direction. "Watch the kid, Lenny."

"Scuse me, Miss," Lenny said.

I scooted away from them. What was I doing here? At least it was warm inside, except the smell of hotdogs and French fries were making my mouth water. The sandwich I'd had that morning seemed a distant memory.

I stared at a nearby food stand where they were grilling burgers, and a vat of grease bubbled with French fries. Out front, a counter held a display of chips, pretzels, and nuts. Hungry customers formed a line before the cash register.

"Uh, excuse me," I said moving next to the guy in the head of the line. "I just want to grab some chips."

He shrugged. I grabbed three little bags of potato chips, and moved to the back of the line. How the hell could I keep these bags without paying? A loud noise caused me to turn. The TV monitors hanging from the ceiling blasted with sound.

"They're off!" the announcer cried as a bell rang and the horses on the monitor exploded from the gate. The crowd turned as one to watch the break. I turned, too, and slid the chips into my pockets. I walked slowly away from the line, expecting to hear cries of "thief!" The only sounds were the announcer calling the race and the bettors shouting for their picks.

I eased around a corner and found a bench on the other side of a divider wall. I felt oddly elated by this second successful theft, and had to suppress a nervous giggle. Sitting on the bench, I ripped open the first bag of chips, scarfing them down so fast, I almost choked on the crumbs. Damn, they tasted good!

But by the time I emptied all three bags, my high had ebbed as the knowledge of what I'd done and the trouble it could bring me left me shaken.

There had to be work I could do on the backstretch. Mom had always said the horse trainers hired illegal immigrants, so why not me?

"I saw you steal those chips."

Staring down at me was the same weird face from four years earlier. The guy with the bleached out skin and black eyes who'd swiped my five-dollar bill at Laurel Park. Now he wore his hair in a Mohawk, with the sides shaved and the top gelled up so it looked like a bleached scrub brush.

He was about eighteen now, bigger and taller. More threatening. It occurred to me he was an albino, except I thought they were supposed to have pale eyes.

Whatever he was, I stood up fast, and walked away. He was bad news. I could hear his jeering laugh behind me.

Rounding the partition, I walked toward the glass wall overlooking the track. A group of horses was parading past, and one of them made me do a double take. It looked like my night time guardian, Silver Punch.

I was confused. Because winter races are run at Laurel, not at Pimlico, I had assumed the track was open only for simulcast betting, but here were the horses on the track going to post. I darted forward, pushed through a set of double doors into the frigid air, and hurried to the rail. A man in a heavy coat and earmuffs held a *Racing Form*. I moved up beside him.

"Excuse me, is horse number seven called Silver Punch?"

"The seven horse?" The man's face was still turned to his *Form*. "Why? You like him?" Then he glanced down at me, his eyes registering surprise. "Hey, you're too young to be betting. Shouldn't you be in school or something?"

"Teacher's conference," I said.

He nodded. "Yeah, his name's Silver Punch. Doctor Braygler owns him. The lady's a plastic surgeon, rich enough to afford some good horses." He glanced at the page again and traced the print with his finger. "He's out of a Two Punch mare. Northern Dancer on top. Got bumped and blocked last time out. He's got a shot in there."

What I didn't know about racing could fill *Wikipedia*. I thought the man was relating Silver Punch's pedigree and what had happened the last time he ran, but wasn't sure. "How come they aren't racing at Laurel?" I asked.

"Water main break. The track's a frozen mess, so they moved racing here until it's fixed."

I pulled on my gloves, put my elbows on the rail, and settled in to watch the race, glad to temporarily forget my troubles. I knew enough to tell from the starting gate's location on the track that the race would be a mile and a quarter and said as much to the man.

"You're and old hand at this stuff, huh?

"I used to come here with my mom a lot."

He smiled. "Yeah, my dad used to bring me. Listen, I'm gonna place a bet on the seven and if he comes in, I'll share it with you."

I shrugged in response, not wanting to be in debt to this guy for any reason. But maybe he was just being nice.

"Hold my spot here," he said. "I'll be back in a minute." He left, and the horses approached the metal starting gate. Members of the gate crew moved out on the track, ready to lead the animals into their respective stalls. About the time the horses were halfway loaded, and Silver Punch stood in the seven slot, the man came back and showed me one of his tickets. He'd bet $30 to win on Silver Punch, and the horse's odds were ten to one against.

I knew from bets Mom had made, that if Punch won, the man would win over $300.

When the horses broke, Silver Punch took the lead. It looked to me like his jockey eased him back to third place and held that position through the first turn and along the backstretch. Into the last turn before the home stretch, the riders got busy whipping and driving their horses.

At the top of the stretch Silver Punch regained his lead, and when he opened up on the others, a little thrill sped through me.

The man wearing earmuffs yelled, "Hi, ho, Silver away!"

He was jumping up and down like a kid, making me smile. Silver Punch motored on, won by about a length and a half, and the man mock-punched my shoulder.

"Kid, you just made us both $150.00! You're my lucky charm!"

I didn't feel like anyone's lucky anything, but if he really meant to give me half the money it would be the best thing that had happened to me in a long time.

"We gotta wait until it's official," he said, watching the board with an anxious eye. No objections were raised, and a moment later when the announcer named Silver Punch the winner, my earmuffed buddy said, "Come on!"

I followed him into the grandstand where he rushed to a betting window and handed in his win ticket. The teller counted out a large wad of green bills and handed it to the man, who in turn counted out $150.00 and held it out to me.

"This is very nice of you, sir. Thank you."

"Lou Bernstein," he said shaking my hand after I slid the money into my coat pocket. "Spend it in good health, dear."

"Thank you, I will," I said, thinking maybe the world wasn't such a bad place after all. Still, I didn't know this man, and needed to be careful. I gave him a brief smile and walked away.

Looking about, I made sure the albino guy wasn't around. The last thing I needed was for him to steal my money again. I hotfooted it into the lady's room to the privacy of a stall, and after leaving a twenty in my pocket, I removed a boot and crammed the rest of the cash into my sock around my ankle. Satisfied that it would be much harder to steal my money, I put the boot on, and returned to the grandstand.

I wanted to see Silver Punch in the winner's circle and hurried through the glass door and onto the track apron. Knowing how long it can take to gallop the winner out and come back to the grandstand, I thought I still had time. I was right. Tense and pumped, the big gray was just being led into the enclosure by the dreadlocked groom I'd met that morning.

The trainer, who'd given me money for food and clothing, stood in the winner's enclosure. A pretty blonde, who must be the owner, Dr. Braygler, was next to him. She had cheekbones like a model and wore a real fur coat. The three of them should have worn huge smiles, but there was something almost wistful in the expressions on the face of the trainer and his groom.

Another groom was standing just outside the circle. When I saw he held a halter and a lead shank, I knew Silver Punch had been claimed. The second groom was a Latino and must work for

Silver Punch's new owner. As soon as the photographer shot the win picture, the Latino would lead the horse away to a different stable, different trainer, and a new owner. I hadn't even realized the horse was running in a claiming race. I wondered how much the new owner had shelled out for the horse.

Suddenly I felt cold and empty. I realized that subconsciously, I'd planned on sneaking back to the horse's stall for the night. Now, he was gone. Every piece of security and comfort had been taken from me. My Mom, my home, Miss Boiler, and now even a stupid horse.

Damn everything.

7

No time to sink into an abyss of self-pity. I had to think about food and shelter.

Paying for a motel was out of the question. I had to hang on to my newfound cash. Besides, a motel would want ID, and I didn't have any. Come to think of it, how had I imagined I could find work without ID?

I felt my spirits sag as fast as the late winter sun that was sliding to the western horizon. As I headed back to the warmth of the grandstand, two cops emerged from the glass door, their eyes searching the crowd.

Stanley knows I love the track. Had he reported me as a runaway? Suggested that I might be found here? Had the albino told someone I stole food?

I turned away from the officers' inquiring gaze, and pulled my hood farther forward until it covered my forehead and partially hid my eyes. I felt myself go rigid as farther up the track apron, I saw two more police officers prowling through the fans. *Everything isn't about you, Nikki. They are probably l looking for a real felon.* But I wasn't taking any chances.

The guy with the dreads had helped the Latino groom switch halters, and now the new man led Silver Punch toward the track. I stole a look toward the two closest cops and saw that they were approaching a small group of racing fans standing behind me. One of the cops held out a photo.

I kept my back to them and listened.

"Have any of you seen this girl?"

"No, sir," one male voice replied.

"What did she do?" a woman's voice asked.

"She's missing." This last voice must have belonged to the cop.

Damn it. I edged toward the winner's circle, where Silver Punch was stepping onto the dirt track. The horse would be led around to the backside and out of my life.

I took a deep breath, stepped through an opening into the enclosure, and followed the horse onto the track like I knew what I was doing.

The Latino groom, who was maybe thirty, gave me a questioning look. His eyes drifted to the cops and back to me. He shrugged and said, "You'd better hurry up, *chica*. This horse, he walks fast."

I jogged to catch up and walked alongside him like it was what I did every day. But my heart raced as I waited for a cop to yell at me to stop. The sound didn't come, and I never looked back.

"Thank you," I said to the groom.

"*De nada.* What is your name?"

"Nikki."

He flashed a smile at me, his white teeth bright against his olive skin. "I am Carlos Pedroza."

He had nice eyes and seemed to have no problem with me tagging along, so I asked where he was taking Silver Punch.

"He go to the barn of Mr. Ravinsky at Laurel."

"What's Mr. Ravinsky like?"

"How you say in Inglés, his bark is worse than his bite?" He nodded as if mentally confirming his words. "And he is very good to the horses."

I was glad Silver Punch was going to a nice home, but by now I was panting from keeping up with Carlos and the horse. I'd never walked on a racetrack before and was dismayed that the sandy surface was so heavy and deep. It seemed like Silver Punch walked faster with each stride.

"You understand," Carlos said, "the horse, he win, he must go to detention barn, yes?"

I didn't understand, but nodded like I knew what he was talking about.

"You will not be allowed in this barn."

I nodded. I didn't know what a detention barn was, but who'd want to go into one, anyway? It sounded like going to jail.

By the time we were close to the backstretch stables, I was sweating inside my down-jacket and felt like collapsing onto the sand. Finally, we stepped off the track onto a more solid dirt path, and Carlos headed toward a barn where a track security guard stood outside.

I eased away and headed for the barn with the diner on the second floor. As I climbed the steps, I saw a police cruiser roll slowly by on the pavement below. I double timed it into the "kitchen, and looked from the window, exhaling with relief when the cruiser kept going and disappeared from sight.

I used some of the twenty-dollar bill in my pocket to buy a cheeseburger, fries, and a Coke, then found an empty chair in the corner. The burger was hot, the cheese melted, the fries crisp. Total heaven. Ravenous, I scarfed it all down, but took my time drinking the Coke. The little grill seemed like a good hiding place for me. At least for the moment.

The door opened and the groom with the dreads walked in. When he saw me, he nodded. I stood, put my empty plate in the trash, and still holding my coke, I walked to the window and looked onto the backstretch below.

"If you're looking for Punch, he'll be in the spit barn," the man said.

"Spit barn?"

"I forgot. You're . . . new here. Don't know much about the track, do you?"

"Not really. I thought Punch had to go to the *detention* barn."

"Spit barn, test barn, detention barn, it's all the same. Most always the horses that run one and two gotta be tested."

"For what?" *Weren't they tested enough in their race?*

"Man, you got a lot to learn. Drugs. They get tested for drugs."

I started to ask him what drugs, but he pursed his lips and shook his head. He brushed past me and went to the counter to order food, then he turned back to me.

"And you'd better stay off our shedrow, too."

Shedrow?

Seeing my bewildered look, he said, "Don't you know anything? Our row of stalls. Our part of the barn. Shit, I ain't running no nursery school." With that, he turned away from me for good.

Why did some people have to be mean? I glanced out the window again. No cops in sight. I figured the security guard was at the detention barn only because of the drug testing. It shouldn't take too long to test a horse for drugs, should it?

I slid my hood over my head and stepped outside into the sharp cold. Keeping an eye out for cops, I walked down the stairs and back to the entrance of the test barn, where I stood watching several horses being led along the aisle inside.

After a couple of minutes Carlos appeared, taking Silver Punch past on the barn aisle like the other grooms had done. As they went by me, a man appeared. He held a long stick with what looked like a large mason jar attached to one end.

He called to Carlos, "Take him in. See if he's ready."

Carlos nodded and led Silver Punch into a stall opposite the entrance. The man with the jar followed behind and closed both the top and bottom stall doors.

I could hear Carlos whistling and then the sound of liquid pouring into the jar. The man came out. His jar was filled with yellow foaming liquid. The horse must have peed in the jar.

No sooner had the jar-man left, than a veterinarian stepped into the stall, pulled out a nasty looking syringe, shoved its needle into Punch's neck, and drew blood.

So the winner had been claimed by a stranger, stuck with a big needle, and then was expected to pee in a jar. What kind of incentive to win was that?

Apparently they were done, because Carlos led Punch from the barn. Would the horse leave for Laurel now? They walked away, heading to the bottom of a steep dirt path leading up to an area overlooking the backstretch stabling. The horse had brought me luck so far. Watching him leave, I felt lost. I broke into a jog and followed them up the hill.

Hearing my footsteps, Carlos glanced back and frowned. "You cannot go with us."

Halfway up the steep hill and out of breath, I stopped, my gaze dropping to my rubber boots that were covered with sandy dirt. *What choice did I have?*

I couldn't go back to Potter's School, I couldn't go home, and now the police were looking for me at Pimlico. I wanted to scream or weep. Instead, I leaned forward and trudged up the hill.

Reaching the top, there were two barns ahead of us. To their right was a paved area. The rattle and smell of a diesel engine filled the air as an eighteen wheeler stood idling next to a dirt bank, which apparently served as a loading ramp for the huge van.

Carlos and Punch disappeared into the closest barn. Gritting my teeth, I stepped from the sunlight into the barn.

At first, I couldn't figure out what was going on inside. Grooms sat or stood outside the thirty some stalls which stretched before of me. Restless horses paced inside each one, and outside, small trunks or cases lined the aisle. They held supplies like bandages and brushes.

The tangy smell of liniment was so strong that if my nose had been stuffy, it would have opened right up. The grooms were mostly male, with varying skin tones from freckled-white to dark-chocolate, with a few women were sprinkled among them.

Everyone stared at me. No one said anything. This must be the crowd that had shipped in from Laurel Park. Now it made sense that Carlos would bring the horse here.

Punch's dark silver tail was just receding into a stall ahead of me, and I hurried forward with no idea of what I'd do next. Carlos came out, scowled when he saw me, but remained silent. He opened his own small trunk, pulled out a set of rolled bandages, and carried them into the stall.

Eventually, Carlos brought Silver Punch out and headed for the barn entrance. I followed as close as I dared as they headed toward the eighteen wheeler. I couldn't follow them, but if I–

A police cruiser nosed into the parking area. Following it was a horribly familiar truck with ladders strapped to the top. A wave of fear crashed through me. *Stanley.* I couldn't move my feet.

The squad car slowed as it neared Carlos and Silver Punch, finally stopping between them and the ramp to the van. The driver's window slid down, and I could see him showing a photo to Carlos.

Carlos shook his head. "No speak English."

He waved one arm in the air and babbled in Spanish. By now, Silver Punch was getting upset and rose into the air in a half rear next to the cop car. The driver eased the car away from the horse. Stanley followed suit, and the two vehicles stopped beyond the horse van.

Carlos spoke softly to Punch, stroking his neck until the animal grew calm. He darted a quick glance at me. I was rooted to the pavement with fear. His eyes shifted to the cruiser and ladder-truck, and then back to me.

"Maria!" he called, looking right at me. He motioned with his hand for me to come. "*Darse prisa!*"

I didn't understand him, but hand motions tend to be universal. I broke through my wall of fear and double timed it to where he stood.

"The *policia,* they look for you?"

"Yes."

The truck's door opened. Stanley climbed out. My knees were shaky and I must have turned white. Carlos stared at Stanley.

"This man, he also look for you?"

I managed to nod.

"You are afraid of him, no?"

"He is a terrible man."

Stanley started walking toward us. Carlos put an arm around my shoulder, turning me away from Stanley. He began babbling in Spanish again. I nodded like I understood every word.

In my peripheral vision Stanley turned away from us and walked toward the barn. Searching for me.

"Hurry. Go in the van." He pushed me toward the dirt bank leading to the side door of the big rig.

A last glance. The two cops walked behind Stanley, all three of their backs to me as they headed for the barn I'd just left. I scooted up the ramp and into the van. There were horses and grooms already inside. Carlos led Silver Punch in behind me, backed him into an empty slot, and snapped tie chains to Punch's halter rings.

A few minutes later, a man with the name of the shipping company on both his jacket and ball cap came up the ramp. He stared at his clipboard, checking off the names of the horses on board.

Sick with fear, I glanced out the van's window, certain I'd see Stanley and the police coming to search inside the van.

I almost sank to my knees with relief when the van man closed the trailer's door. I held my breath until the big rig lurched forward as the cab shifted into first gear. Slowly, we inched our way out of the parking area. I stole another peek outside.

Stanley stood in the barn entrance, his hands on his hips, his eyes searching the parking lot. He looked angry.

Carlos stepped next to me and stared at Stanley. His teeth flashed white as he grinned.

"That man, he not hurt you again."

I tried to return his smile. "*Gracias,* Carlos."

I had no idea where I was going next or what would happen to me, but for the moment, I was safe.

8

About an hour later, the tractor trailer wheeled through the security gates of Laurel and labored through the backstretch, before finally stopping. When the van door opened, we were parked next to another dirt platform where the grooms unloaded their horses.

Walking down the sandy ramp behind Silver Punch, I could see the racetrack's final turn curving before me. In the distance, the grandstand where I'd watched so many races with Mom, loomed against the sky. Barns, sheds, and outbuildings filled the rest of the grounds as far as I could see.

The euphoria of escaping Baltimore and Stanley faded as renewed apprehension raced through me. What would I do now?

Tucking in behind Silver Punch, I followed him onto a paved section. The road wound past a building set so it overlooked Laurel's final turn. Exhaust fans blew the smell of fried food into the air, telling me the building must be the track kitchen. I may have had the burger and fries at Pimlico, but as the winter daylight faded and an icy breeze kicked up, I was hungry again.

The door to the kitchen opened and a figure emerged. Mostly hidden by a parka, the man's face was hard to see. He turned my way briefly. Pale, colorless skin, white eyebrows, and black eyes. I forgot about food and hurried to catch up with Silver Punch. I thought I'd left the albino at Pimlico, but my knotted insides told me he was here.

Carlos ignored several barns we passed on our left, staying on the path that followed the curve of the track's rail. The massive oval and infield spread into the distance to our right. As we reached what appeared to be the last two barns, a woman called out sharply and ran toward Carlos.

She had the short waist and sturdy body often seen in Mexican women. Her round face was torn by anxiety.

"No puedo en contrar a Pedro!" Her voice rose to a shriek on the name Pedro.

Carlos responded in a rapid stream of Spanish. I had no idea what they were saying, but it was obvious that something about this Pedro disturbed them greatly. I heard the word *"policia"* more than once and Carlos called the woman "Maria."

Their anxious voices and Maria's waving arms were making Silver Punch nervous. Carlos finally realized it, and urged the horse toward one of the last two barns, quickly getting the animal inside the shedrow railing and leading him into a stall.

The woman remained outside the rail, her palms pressed together before her mouth, tears running down her cheeks. Carlos left the stall in a rush, one hand clenched in a fist. When he saw me standing in his shedrow, he frowned.

Before he could tell me to get lost, I asked, "Is there anything I can do to help?"

He made an impatient noise and started to speak, but Silver Punch snorted, whirled, and slammed his chest into the stall gate. Instinctively, I spoke soft, reassuring nonsense. The horse paused, pricked his hears, and stared at me. His head came down and his wild eyes appeared to soften.

"Yes," Carlos said, finally responding to my question. "Stay here. Keep the horse calm. I must go. Our son, he is missing."

"Oh, I hope you . . ." But Carlos was already hurrying away from the barn with Maria at his side.

I sagged against Silver Punch's stall gate as the trauma that had stalked me for three long days took its toll. Running away from Stanley that first night, escaping to Pimlico's backside, sleeping in a stall, and then running from Stanley again the following day.

I closed my eyes against these unpleasant thoughts, but it was no use. I could hear the ugly laugh of the albino who'd taunted me at Pimlico, see the cops who'd looked for me on the track apron, and feel long trek across the deep racetrack, and the cold van ride from Laurel.

I shivered at the memory of the albino's reappearance, and the terrible distress I'd seen in Carlos' eyes, a man I'd started to trust and like.

Silver Punch pulled me back to the present when he snorted and started pacing anxiously. I slipped under the stall gate and put my hands on his neck. He leaned into me, sending his strength and energy into my fingertips. This is where I belonged.

Settling on the floor, I curled into a ball next to Silver Punch's hay flakes, pulled my hood over my head, and closed my eyes tight. I had one talent—I could ride. Why couldn't I ride racehorses? It was my last thought before I fell asleep.

"Did you come with the horse?"

The words awakened me. I sat up quickly, alarmed. A tall man with bushy gray brows framing his eyes was staring at me. His frame was bent by age, and gray wisps of hair poked from under a cap that said "Meyers Feed."

I didn't know what to say. Silent, I stared at his knotty fingers. They curled through the wire squares of the stall gate as he stood outside watching me.

"Speak up. Who are you?"

"Nikki. I–"

"Where's Carlos?"

"His son, Pedro, is missing."

"Damn." He shook his head, tapped one finger against his lip. "You a friend of Carlos?"

"Sort of. I was watching Silver Punch while he went to look for Pedro."

"And here I thought you were asleep. Did Maria go with him?" When I nodded, he said, "Come on out of there." Unlatching the gate, he held it ajar for me.

I slipped through and was about to scurry away when he gently grasped my shoulder.

"Since Carlos and Maria are missing, you want to help me feed?"

"Sure," I said relieved he wasn't throwing me out or waylaying me until track security arrived.

"Jim Ravinsky." He stuck out a gnarled hand.

I shook it, and looked into his face. Though his demeanor was stiff and somewhat gruff, there was kindness in his eyes. "You're the trainer, right?"

"Yes. What's your last name, Nikki?"

I told him, and he said, "Come on, then."

I followed him past three more stalls to the end of the long rectangular barn. Around the corner, at the short end, there were no stalls. Instead, there were doors, behind which I soon discovered, were a feed room, a tack room, and an office.

On the opposite wall, bales of timothy hay and straw piled high against the cinder block walls. There was a short stack of deep green alfalfa that smelled sweet and fragrant even from a distance.

Inside the feed room, were bags of oats, sweet feed, and bran. A number of jugs and containers labeled with words like flax seed oil, Source, Bigeloil, and Uptite lined one wall.

"I got eight horses on that shedrow. You can tell mine by the red and green webbing." He gave me a piercing look, as if to make sure I was listening.

"Yes sir," I said, remembering the metal chains coated with heavy red and green rubber that were fastened across every stall but Silver Punch's. That must be the webbing.

"Use this," he said, holding up a battered coffee tin. "Give each horse one and a half cans of whole oats." He pointed at a large bag leaning against the wall. "And a can of sweet feed, that's this bag, and a half can of bran." He pointed at a large burlap bag.

"Each time you measure, dump the can into a different one of those eight pails. When you're done, you're gonna add hot water to each bucket and stir it into a bran mash."

"Yes sir." I hesitated about asking, but curiosity won out. "How come you don't just use bags of premixed feed? Don't they sell that for racehorses?"

The old man reared back as if offended. "I'm not letting some company moron with a fancy degree set *my* feed. Probably some kid never stepped on a backstretch." He shook his head in disgust before continuing.

"I know what to feed by how they look, how they act, the glow in their eyes and the shine on their coats. Now start scooping."

"Yes, sir." I wouldn't be questioning his methods again any time soon. He'd almost bitten my head off. I was hoping he'd leave the feed room, but he walked to the single chair in the room and lowered himself to sit on it and watch me. With his stiff gray brows above each eye, and his hard stare, he reminded me of a hawk.

One and a half oats, one half sweet, one half bran. I silently repeated the recipe as I went to work, scared to death I'd mix it up.

When I got it done, he handed me a five-gallon bucket. "There's a spigot outside. Fill this and bring it back here."

I found the spigot, filled the bucket, but was dismayed by how much it weighed. As I hobbled along the dirt aisle with it, the bucket bumped against one leg and splashed water down one thigh, calf and into my rubber boot. *Damn, it was cold.*

"Set that down."

I did. Ravinsky had come from the feed room to check my progress. "Surprised you could lift it at all," he said, with the ghost of a smile on his mouth. "At least you got spunk. Little muscle, too, from the look of it."

"I ride a lot," I said, wanting him to know it.

"Where?"

"Potter's School."

Confusion clouded his eyes, and he tapped a finger against his lips. "*You* go to Potter's School?"

He knew there was no way a stray kid in need of a bath, a comb, and a toothbrush was a Potter student.

"No sir. I work, I mean worked in the stables. They let me ride."

"So what brings you here, Nikki?"

"I, well, my mother . . ." Oh hell, I was going to cry. Ravinsky didn't want some tearful teenager in his barn. Wasn't interested in my troubles. I took a breath. "Um, I–"

"Spit it out, girl. Do your parents know where you are?"

"I don't have any." Too late. The tears were running down my face, and my nose had turned into a wet faucet. A sob wracked me.

"Oh for God's sake," Ravinsky said. He grabbed a small towel from the wood railing and handed it to me."

"Thank you," I said, turning away from him to blow my nose and mop my face.

"You might as well tell me your story," he said. "You can't work here if I don't know what's going on with you."

So I told him. Told him everything, finishing with, "I won't go back to Stanley!"

"And how do I know you didn't make all this up?"

Anger hit me. "Mom's obituary is in the Baltimore Sun. Look it up online. I'm not lying!"

He raised a placating hand. "Okay, okay. So the immediate problem is where you're going to stay tonight, right?"

The indignation drained out of me. "Yes sir."

We got an extra room next to my office. It's got a cot and blankets in it. Little heater, too. You can stay there tonight until we figure out what to do with you."

"Yes sir," I said, biting my lip to keep from weeping over this unexpected kindness.

He lifted the bucket effortlessly, and carried it into the feed room.

"Well, come on then. I haven't got all day."

I hurried after him, wondering if my luck had finally changed.

9

When I got inside the feed room, Ravinsky was sliding a metal heating rod into the five gallon bucket of water. He plugged it into a wall socket, and before long, steam rose into the cold air.

"Hand me a pail," he said.

I did, and watched his bent frame lean over the steaming water. His knotty hands ladled liquid into the pail and then stirred the feed into a mash with a stick. He reminded me of an ancient wizard at a cauldron, his magical potion filling the air with the sweet smell of molasses, oats, and bran.

A footstep sounded in the doorway. Carlos was back, his face tight with anxiety. He looked defeated and very tired.

"I'm sorry, Papa," he said to Ravinsky. "But my son, he is missing."

"When did you see him last?"

"This morning. He left to work the lunch at Burrito Burro, but he no come home. And the people there, they say he leave at two. We check his friends. No one knows where he is." He held his hands out, palms up, his expression grim. "Pedro, he is not that kind of boy. We always know where he is. He *always* come home!

I was afraid Carlos might break down in tears. I hated the pain in his eyes and wished I could help. If the son had a job working at the well-known chain restaurant that served Mexican food, wouldn't somebody there know *something*?

Ravinsky ladled water into another feed pail and kept stirring. "You said the boy was worried about something. Ever find out what?"

"No. He not tell us. Maria, she is very upset!"

"You call the police?"

"Yes, but they say he must be missing twenty-four hours. Is stupid rule. They should look for him *now*!"

Ravinsky grabbed another pail and kept mixing. "Nikki, you good to keep helping?"

"Of course."

"Okay. Carlos, you go on and look for your boy. We'll take care of things here."

"Carlos," I said as he started to leave. "Do you have a picture of Pedro?"

"*Sí.*" He pulled a wallet from his winter jacket and extracted a small photo. "Is from school. Last year

I gazed at the picture. A good looking, dark-haired kid with cherub lips and warm eyes smiled back at me. He wore a silver chain with a patron saint medal around his neck.

"He's really cute," I said, feeling my cheeks flush with embarrassment. "He doesn't look any older than me."

"He's thirteen."

"*Oh.* I'll keep an eye out for him," I said, feeling a rush of empathy for Pedro. I knew a lot about being thirteen, in trouble, and alone.

"*Gracias.*" Carlos took the photo back before turning from me and hurrying away to search for his son.

Ravinsky had finished mixing hot water into the eight pails. Now he grabbed some of the jugs and cartons and began sprinkling and pouring small amounts of stuff into each pail.

"Take these first two," he said, gesturing at the line of pails, and dump the grain into the feed tub in the first two stalls. Mind you're quick about it, or they'll shove their heads into your pail and knock it on the floor. They suffer over eagerness at feeding time."

"Yes sir."

I managed to get the contents of eight pails into the feed tubs without getting bitten or stepped on, but wound up with a sprinkling of sticky grain on my clothes, in the pockets of my coat, and my hair.

I liked Ravinsky. He struck me as a kind, decent man, and I prayed he'd let me work for him at Laurel. As I moved down the line of stalls, I wondered about Pedro. Had he run away from home? Was he hurt? I might have thought he was just hanging with friends, except his parents found his absence so unusual and alarming.

It was nice to worry about someone other than myself. But as the winter night sky darkened outside the barn and the cold air grew more frigid, a familiar feeling of panic overtook me.

You have a safe place to sleep tonight. Just keep going, Nikki. You can do this.

When I got to my room, it was warm and toasty. Once again I curled up in my cot with the comforting scent of horses, sweet feed, and the tangy, clean smell of liniment.

My last thoughts before I went to sleep were about Pedro. Maybe if the Mexican restaurant where he worked was close by, I'd go there for lunch. I wanted to do something to help Carlos. It was probably a dumb idea, but I couldn't shake it.

I slept soundly, amazed to wake up and find the gray light of another cold dawn coming through the dusty window of my room. It was the first time I'd slept through the night since Stanley had come into my life.

I worked hard that morning. Feeding the eight horses and cleaning out their stalls while each one was exercising out on the track. I felt a little in awe and envious of the two small and wiry Latino guys that showed up to ride. They wore cool-looking leather chaps and boots as they rode the horses off the shedrow and headed for the sandy mile-oval, something I was longing to do.

"Do the horses gallop every day?" I asked Ravinsky.

"Yep," he said. "Except if they've just had a race. We usually give them three days off. Just walk them around the shedrow to let them stretch their legs a bit."

"So Silver Punch will just walk today?"

"Yep. But he worries me a bit, 'cause he didn't eat his feed and hardly any hay. Course that's not unusual to back off right after a race. Let's hope he cleans up his dinner."

Then he studied my face and nodded as if he'd reached a decision. "I'll need you to help Maria walk 'em as soon as you're done cleaning the stalls."

"Yes sir."

Apparently he was still figuring out what to do with me, as he worked me hard, but not unfairly. He'd brought me a box of fried chicken, coleslaw, and biscuits the night before and I'd wolfed it down so fast, he'd mumbled something about a stray cat.

As I continued working, Maria showed up looking drawn and pale, shaking her head when Ravinsky asked her about Pedro.

"He never came home."

"It will be twenty-four hours soon," Ravinsky said, "The police will start looking for him."

For some reason this made Maria take an involuntary step back. Then she shuttered the sudden fear I'd seen on her face.

"Where can they look more than Carlos? He is still searching. I am sorry Carlos is not here for you."

"Don't worry about it. Nikki's doing a good job on the stalls."

Maria flashed me a grateful smile.

As I finished the stalls, I thought how much I liked the long braid of shiny black hair that hung down her back halfway to her waist. Her full face would be pretty if she was happy. When I was done, she showed me the ropes for hot walking a horse, which were more complicated than I'd expected.

I had to constantly watch each horse as I walked him, checking to see how hot and wet his coat was, how much water he was allowed to drink and when. What surprised me the most was that after he drank most of his water and was almost cooled out, I was expected to take him in his stall and encourage him to pee by whistling.

Then I remembered that only the day before, which seemed more like half a lifetime ago, Carlos had done the same thing with Silver Punch after the horse won at Pimlico.

By the time Maria and I were finished, it was almost eleven a.m. Hungry, I asked Maria where the Mexican restaurant was.

She told me it was on 198, within walking distance, and gave me directions.

"Hold on a minute," Ravinsky said when he got wind of my plan. "How do you think you're going to get back in here without a license badge to show the gate guard?"

Oops, dumb not to realize that if I went out, I couldn't get back in unless I wanted to climb more razor wire. "I, I don't know."

"I'm leaving shortly. I'll drive you up to the gate and get you a three-day pass. But after I put you on my badge list, you'll need to go to the racing commission office in the grandstand. Give them your ID and social security number and they'll issue you a hot walker's license.

Maybe now wasn't the time to tell him I didn't have a social security number, was too young to have a driver's license, and my birth certificate was in Baltimore in the house with Stanley. *No way* was I *going back there.*

Ravinsky headed into his office, and Maria, who'd been listening to the conversation, motioned me to walk down the shedrow with her. A few steps later, she stopped and looked around as if to make sure no one was listening.

"You have your ID?"

When I told her no, she said, "There is a man, he is assistant manager at Burrito Burro. He help some of us. His name is Bic.

Give him my name, Maria Pedroza. He can get you a Social
Security card."

"A fake one?"

"*Sí,*" she said, with a worried glance up and down the
shedrow, obviously worried someone might overhear.

"How much?"

"Not too bad," she said. "Maybe fifty dollars."

I'd already doled out more of my win money than I'd meant
to, but if I wanted to work, this would be money well spent.
Unless I got caught.

"*Sí,*" she said, with a worried glance up and down the
shedrow, obviously worried someone might overhear.

"Won't the racing commission guy know it's fake?"

"No. My brother, he got work here." Then she pressed her lips
together in a way that suggested she'd said more than she'd meant
to.

"I won't say anything," I said. "Thank you, Maria." If I'd had
doubts about checking the place Pedro was last seen, the lure of
obtaining an ID overrode my hesitation.

I started to walk away, and then turned back. "Maria, what
did Pedro do at the restaurant?"

"He worked in the kitchen. He cut the peppers and tomatoes,
stir the sauce pots."

Like Mom.

"You find anything," Maria said, "you let me know, yes?"

"Of course."

A while later I was driven off the grounds by Ravinsky in his
Ford 250 pickup. He hung a right on Whiskey Bottom Road,
and another right on Brock Bridge Road which paralleled the
backstretch barns to our right. He reached a stoplight at the four
lane highway that was198.

Pulling close to the curb, he withdrew his wallet. "Here's for
today's work," he said, extracting a fifty-dollar bill.

I slipped the money into my pocket. "Thank you."

"Hop out here," he said. "Restaurant's in a strip mall about a block away. You might want the drugstore that's there, or the Goodwill a little farther down."

He must have been reading my thoughts. I'd been longing for a toothbrush, shampoo, soap, towels, and a trip to the backstretch shower.

When I reached the strip mall, I saw a billboard above a restaurant picturing a donkey with a basket of burritos on his back. A happy, smiling man in a serape and Mexican hat led the burro. The burro wasn't smiling

Pushing through the glass door, I almost felt faint when I was hit by the aroma of cooked beef, chili sauce, and beans. Investigating what had become of Pedro and the search for a fake ID would have to wait until I'd consumed at least two tacos.

The restaurant was the downscale type where you go to the counter, order, pay, and then someone brings the food to your table. The floor tiles were the color of terra cotta and the walls were decorated with murals of the same burro and man on the billboard outside.

Two Latina women worked there behind the counter and apparently a skinny little guy who emerged through a swinging door with a tray of hot chili sauce.

I ordered three tacos, and when I'd finished them, I went back to the counter and spoke to the women behind it.

"I'm looking for my friend, Pedro. Is he in today

One woman looked away from me, and the other said, "No, he's not here."

"Well, have you seen him?"

The woman lowered her voice as two customers entered the shop. "He's missing. Never showed up today, never called. He's in hot water with the boss, I'll tell you that.

"So, you have no idea where I can find him?"

"No, I don't." Her gaze slid to the new customers. "May I help you?"

The two newcomers said they wanted to read the wall menu first, so I asked the woman, "What about Bic. Is he in today?"

Her expression changed, her body seemed to still momentarily, and she stiffened. "Yeah, he's here."

"May I speak with him? Tell him Maria Pedroza sent me."

Her friendly attitude evaporated. "I'll see." She walked out from behind the counter, down a short hall past the restrooms, and knocked on a door at the end.

She came back, gestured at the now open door. "In there."

I walked to the doorway and went inside. A beige wall lined with file cabinets faced me. To my right was a metal desk, with a laptop and a bunch of papers. A guy sitting in an office chair behind it raised his head to look at me.

He might as well have been a snake, coiled and ready to strike, because seeing him stopped me dead.

10

I stared at the albino, at the black holes where warm eyes should have been. I had to remind myself to breathe.

Recognition flickered across his face. His mouth twisted into a condescending shape somewhere between a smirk and a smile.

"You come here to steal food?"

He was such a jerk! But I couldn't raise enough contempt to drown my fear. Was it because his eyes had no soul?

I had to swallow before I could get the words out. "I need ID."

"I bet you do," he said. "So, you know Maria?"

"Yeah. She told me to see you. I, uh, I need a social security card so I can work in her barn." I hated asking this guy for *anything*.

"He leaned back in his desk chair, folded his arms across his chest. "Small world, huh? That no good son of hers ever show up?"

"I don't know anything about that," I said. "I have money. I need ID. Can you help?"

"You seem to have a lot of problems. What happened to your mommy?"

So the jerk remembered stealing my five dollars and how I'd run back to Mom in tears.

"She's dead."

At least he had the decency to look startled. "Sorry for your loss."

Then his eyes narrowed and a calculating expression crossed his face. "So you're on your own now?"

I nodded.

"Sure, I can help you out. I'll need twenty-five today. Come back tomorrow. I'll have the card and you can pay me another twenty-five."

Just like that? "Don't you need my name or something?"

"Hell no, I can't use your real name."

His eyes kept moving rapidly back and forth as if he had no control over them. And when he looked at me, he seemed to have trouble training both eyes on me at once. If he hadn't been such a bully, I might have felt sorry for him.

"So," I asked, "what name will you use?"

"Some dead lady's." Then he laughed like he'd just told a great joke.

The beige walls of the office seemed to close in on me, and I took a breath, trying to stay calm. What a horrible man Pedro worked for. How could Maria stand it?

Then it hit me. The whole Pedroza family was probably in the country illegally. That's why Ravinksy's mention of the police had made Maria so nervous. Did Ravinksy know? But what if he did? *This isn't your concern, Nikki.*

"So you got the twenty-five or what," Bic said leaning forward, making the desk chair groan.

I had put fifty dollars in my pocket earlier and pulled out a twenty and a five, placing it in his outstretched hand.

"Come back same time tomorrow," he said. "I'll have it for you."

I wanted to get out of there. "Okay," I said, before turning on my heel and forcing myself not to run from his office.

Outside the restaurant, I walked past its glassed-in front, stopped before the hardware store next door, and let out a long breath.

Why did this guy have to turn out to be the freaking albino?

I'd known he was a creep, but even when he'd stolen my five that day, I'd only thought of him as a bully. But here he was providing false ID. He was a *criminal*. Who knew what else he might be into?

Had anyone pressed *him* if he knew anything about what happened to Pedro? Maria and Carlos were probably afraid to ask if they were illegals and he'd provided their ID.

It's none of your business. You're in enough trouble already.

Still, I found myself walking to the end of the block and around the corner where I found a wide alley running behind the restaurant. Maybe there was some trace or sign of Pedro. Maybe I could find *something*. Heading into it, I passed numerous locked steel doors and garbage cans. At my feet were frozen puddles of dirty water imbedded with grit, trash, and cigarette butts.

Halfway down, I found the back door of Burrito Burro. It had a small loading dock with a Dumpster to one side. So far I was accomplishing nothing.

Turning in a slow circle, I surveyed the signage on the back entrances of the buildings lining the alley. There was the hardware store, a print shop, an auto parts store, and a beauty salon.

The door directly across from Burrito Burro's appeared to be the back entrance to a doctor's office. The building used a lot of space, stretching to the far end of the alley. The name Braygler was stenciled on the rear door. I'd heard the name before. But where? I couldn't remember.

A wind kicked up at the head of the alley and I pulled my coat closer around me. This was stupid. I wasn't learning anything other than how freaking cold it was in the alley. I walked back to 198 and hit the drug store and Goodwill.

After purchasing necessities at the first stop and some jeans and two fleece shirts at the second, I headed for the racetrack. When I saw the barns just behind the fence on Whiskey Bottom Road, my spirits lifted. I knew that inside each building, there were horses bedded deep in straw, wearing warm blankets, enjoying an abundance of hay, feed, and water. I'd found a place where I belonged. Well, almost belonged.

I showed my day pass to the guard at the stable gate, and then trudged along the paved road past a number of barns and a big lot filled with horse trailers and vans. Beyond that was the biggest barn on the grounds, which I'd learned was the receiving barn, which is to say it *received* the horses that were shipping in for that day's races.

Walking along, I passed shedrows with multi colored bandages hanging on the railing to dry in the cold sun. Salsa music drifted from some of the stables, but it was the occasional ring of a hoof, or the sound of a snort, or whinny that was music to my ears.

A rooster and three hens were scratching in the grass nearby. I'd never seen a real chicken before coming to this backstretch. Apparently trainers kept them for eggs or just because they liked having them around. The birds were colorful additions, and I found their behavior to be both ridiculous and endearing.

When I reached Ravinksy's barn, I went into my room, loving the heat emanating from the room's little electric heater. I had just set my parcels down on the bed when someone knocked on my door.

It was Maria. She stared at me, the tension in her body indicating her desperation for good news.

"Did you hear anything at the restaurant?"

"No, Maria. I'm sorry. I didn't." The way her face fell made me feel like I'd just kicked a dog. "I asked the women behind the counter. They didn't know anything about Pedro."

"Did you see Bic?"

"I did. Thank you for telling me about him. He's going to help me," I said.

"Did you ask Bic about my Pedro?"

"No, he . . . I was afraid to ask him."

"*Sí. Yo comprendo.* He is not a nice man."

My curiosity about Bic was as strong as my uneasiness about him. *I* knew he wasn't a nice man. But what did she know?

"Is he mean to Pedro?"

"Sometimes. But he cheated us. He took our money. Said he would help with immigration. But he do nothing."

My face must have given away my thoughts, because she said, "Don't worry. You will get your card. *That* he will do."

"What is Bic's last name?" I asked, thinking I could look him up on Ravinsky's laptop.

"His last name?" Her brows pulled together as she tried to remember. "*Un momento.* Let me think."

I didn't know much, but it seemed odd that a guy around eighteen would know anything about immigration. Maybe there would be information about him online that could help Carlos and Maria to get their money back. Sometimes on Mom's computer I'd found "beware" sites about people and the bad things they'd done.

Carlos and Maria had been so nice to me; I longed to do *something* to help them.

"Braygler," Maria said suddenly. "Braygler is his last name."

The name I'd heard before but hadn't been able to remember where. And today I had seen it again, stenciled on the backdoor of a doctor's office.

"Does Bic have family in Laurel?" I asked.

"I don't know. Why?"

"I'm just wondering what the deal is with him."

"Well, don't wonder too much. After he give you ID, stay away from him."

Later that afternoon I left my room to visit Silver Punch, and was discouraged to see he'd hardly touched his grain. His hay rack was still full, too. Inside his stall, I stroked his neck and pressed my face close so I could breathe in his horsey smell.

"What's the matter with you, Punch, you homesick?"

If he missed his home and his buddies, I knew just how he felt. I ran my hands over his coat. He was so pretty, his muscles so sculpted. What would it be like to ride a horse like him?"

I slipped out to the aisle to where I'd seen an empty plastic manure bucket. Grabbing its handle, I brought it into the stall. I did this slowly because the last thing I wanted was to startle Silver Punch. I flipped the bucket upside down, put it next to the horse's left side, and slowly stood on it.

Silver Punch turned his head toward me as if curious, but he stood still. Leaning forward I put my hands on his withers and hopped on his back.

He moved into a fast walk, circling his stall. He humped his back once, threatening to buck. I spoke to him softly and stroked his neck. He stopped and turned his neck and head until his nose was on my foot. I giggled, and he walked to his hay net, and pulled out a long wisp.

"Good boy," I said, as I heard the comforting sound of his molars grinding the hay.

He swallowed and grabbed more hay. I bent forward onto his neck and pressed my lips against his silky, grey coat.

"I see you got him eating."

I was appalled to see my boss. "I'm sorry, Mr. Ravinsky! I'll get off. I didn't mean any harm."

"Stay right where you are," he said.

There might have been an amused twitch at the edges of his mouth. Still, I'd gotten on his horse without permission and was terrified he'd order me out of his barn.

"Horse seems to like you. You stay on him and let him eat that hay. I'll get a little fresh grain and see if we can interest him in that."

In no time at all, Punch finished the half pail of grain that Ravinsky brought, and was digging back into his hay.

"Find what works," Ravinsky said. "Any race tracker worth his salt will tell you that." His lips compressed as he shook his head.

"Some horses you can spend months trying to figure out and never get it right."

As he watched his colt eat, light seemed to build in Ravinsky's eyes "But you got his number. Horse just wants company. Maybe he had a companion goat before, or a favorite groom he's missing. But his previous people won't tell us. The last thing they want is for me to be more successful with this horse than they were."

There was a time I would have wondered how Punch's former people could be that mean. But I'd learned some things about the human race since Mom died, and not too much surprised me anymore.

Maria and Carlos showed up late that afternoon for the evening feed and to give the stalls what Ravinsky called a "lick and a promise." It would hold them over until they were cleaned the following morning.

Both grooms seemed to have aged, their faces lined with worry, their eyes filled with despair. When Maria emerged from one stall dragging a manure bucket, tears ran down her face.

She set her bucket down and fingered her tears away with one hand, while the other clutched and twisted a medallion around her neck.

"That's a pretty necklace," I said. It looks like the one in Pedro's picture."

"It is Saint Nicholas, the patron saint of children." She stifled a sob as more tears slid down her face.

I hated that there was nothing I could do to help her. I still wanted to look up Bic on the internet. Maybe I could learn something. When I asked Ravinsky about it, he said he'd bring in his laptop in the morning.

After feeding Silver Punch, I learned that as long as I remained by his stall door, he'd work on his feed. When he cleaned up the last speck of grain, it was the only bright spot of the evening.

Cold and tired from more physical labor than I was used to, I crawled beneath the blankets of my cot early that night. Though Laurel was hardly a "gated community" like you'd see in an upscale real estate ad, I was safe and warm here. I fell asleep immediately.

Sometime in the middle of the night, I sat straight up in bed trying to escape the lingering cobwebs of a nightmare. I'd been dreaming about Pedro. I'd seen his face, his cherub lips, and the medal of a patron saint around his neck. But as I'd tried to reach him, his eyes had turned into the black holes of the albino.

11

In the morning, Silver Punch nickered for his breakfast, ate it right up, and licked his feed tub clean. I liked knowing I'd helped him. That I'd helped Ravinsky. It made me feel more whole inside, even happy.

Still, the dismal cloud of Pedro's disappearance chased after me, and when my chores were finished, I went to the boss's office to use his computer.

His wooden desk was piled with condition books for tracks like Laurel, PARX racing near Philadelphia, and Charles Town in West Virginia. Ravinsky had told me he sometimes shipped horses to the out-of-state tracks, ran a race, and returned the same day.

I picked up one of the books, and realized a trainer could use it to find the conditions which suited a particular horse in his barn. My eyes felt like crossing as I read the differing rules and qualifications. I was particularly confused by the expression "Non winners of a race other than." I gave up trying to figure out what a "starter allowance" was. I had a lot to learn.

My gaze traveled over the rest of the desk. A box of chocolate glazed doughnuts, a broken halter, and a stack of vet and blacksmith bills littered the surface. I grabbed a doughnut and glanced through the bills while I ate. The amount of the vet invoices astonished me. Racehorse owners must have a lot of money.

When I finished my pastry, I licked my fingers and wiped them on my jeans, not wanting to get the sticky residue on Ravinsky's computer keys.

I sat in his chair, powered up his laptop, and Googled the name Bic Braygler. Nothing came up. I'd known it was a longshot, but was still frustrated by the lack of information.

As soon as I earned enough money, I'd buy a smart phone so I could access the internet when I wanted, and contact my friends, Letitia and Carmen. I knew they wouldn't give my location away, and I longed to talk to them. Then my thoughts slid to my mom, how much I missed her, my friends, Boiler, and Potter's School. My emotions were spiraling downward.

I sat up straight, gave myself a mental head smack, and Googled the last name "Braygler," and "Laurel, MD." Damn if the name "Dr. Vivian Braygler, Plastic Surgery Associates" wasn't staring me right in the face!

Of course. She was the woman I'd seen at the track who owned Silver Punch before he was claimed by Ravinsky. Dollars to doughnuts she was related to Bic. And her office was right behind Bic's restaurant, the last place Pedro had been seen. Did this mean anything? I had no idea, but found it very curious.

I continued scrolling under her name and found a news article about her from the local newspaper. Reading it, I learned that Vivian was the franchise owner of Burrito Burro, which meant Bic worked for her.

They had to be related. She was a racehorse owner, which might explain why I kept seeing Bic at the track. Maybe it was a family thing. Since she wielded a scalpel, I hoped she treated people better than her weirdo relative did.

The sound of footsteps made me glance up to see Ravinsky entering the office. I didn't want to hog his chair, so I rose to my feet.

"Find what you were looking for?" he asked.

"Sort of. Mr. Ravinsky, do you know the lady who used to own Silver Punch?"

"You're making me feel ancient with the Mr. Ravinsky. Call me Jim."

"Okay," I said. "But what about this Braygler lady?"

"I don't know her, but expect she may be the best of the lot."

"You mean there's a bunch of Braygler's?"

"Yeah, there's a whole nest of 'em in Laurel. There's a hay-and-feed man, a blacksmith, and then that albino fellow."

"Bic," I said.

A sour look crossed Jim's face. "Yeah, that one."

I told him about Burrito Burro being right across the alley from the Plastic Surgery office, and that Bic was the assistant manager. I figured Jim didn't need to know his employees were obtaining false IDs from the guy.

He rubbed his lips for a moment, as he considered the information. "I think Bic's her nephew. He's a screw up, so she probably felt she had to give him a job."

"How's he a screw up?"

"The physical condition he has is no fun. Albinos usually have vision and socialization problems. He was probably teased and picked on by everyone when he was little. I heard he has a juvenile record for violence. Had to be placed in a special school."

I nodded, not surprised to hear it.

Jim waved his hand in dismissal. "That's enough about the Brayglers. I want to see you get on Wilson's pony."

What?

Wilson was the trainer on the backside of our barn. He had a paint horse that was called a pony as he was used to "pony" or lead racehorses to the track. Ponies made great companions for fractious and nervous Thoroughbreds.

I was dying to ride, but why did Jim want *me* to get on the pony? The suggestion had startled me, and it must have shown on my face.

"I liked the way you sat on Punch. Relaxed and natural. Think we could turn you into an exercise rider one day?"

"Oh my God, I would *love* that!"

I followed him to the tack room where he grabbed an exercise saddle, before walking to the other side of the barn. The pony, whose name was Grit, had a bridle hanging outside his stall.

"Let me see you tack him up," Jim said.

I did, and in no time, Jim gave me a leg up, and I was riding the horse down the shedrow. Since it was after training hours and they still weren't racing at Laurel, there were no other horses out. I had the dirt aisles to myself. When I rounded the corner, Jim had moved to the far end on the other side and his hawk eyes watched me as I rode toward him.

"Stop," he said when I got close.

As soon as I did, he told me to back up. That accomplished, he had me walk on and the next time I came around the corner, he told me to trot Grit toward him. That went well, and after another circuit, he had us ease into a canter.

Stall doors and curious horse heads zipped by us, and the quick rhythm of the animal under me was wonderfully familiar. I knew I was grinning like a fool. I couldn't help it. Riding always gave me a high.

"Keep going," Jim called to me. "Twice more."

Grit was getting cranked up and I had to rein him in a little. He responded until the last time around when a bantam rooster scuttled out of a stall, squawking and flapping his wings right in our path. Grit bucked once, kicked at the chicken as we flew by, and then tried to break into a gallop. I stood in the stirrups, got the leverage I needed, and reined him in.

"All right then, Nikki," Jim said when I pulled up. "We know you can ride. Now you have to learn to gallop a race horse."

I was breathing a little hard, and Jim put a hand on the left rein and walked us down the shedrow.

"I've got a friend who needs a rider," he said. "He's got a half-mile track on his farm. Maybe we can get you up there next week and let him show you the ropes."

"I can't learn here?"

"Nope. Got to be sixteen to go on the big track."

"Oh." Whatever disappointment I felt was whisked away by the thrill of the chance to become an exercise rider. It was the first step toward my dream of being a jockey.

"You should put Grit away and give him a good brushing."

I did, and when I checked my watch I realized it was time to go to Burrito Burro and see Bic. I dreaded the visit, but once he handed me that social security card, I'd be outta there *so* fast, and hopefully never have to see him again.

Without a lift to 198, it was a long trek to the restaurant. I spent the walk through the backstretch daydreaming about being a jockey. As I passed through the stable gate onto Race Track Road a cloud bank darkened the western horizon as a bitterly cold wind kicked up.

The air smelled damp and above me the gloomy sky appeared leaden. Shivering, I zipped my coat up to my chin and pulled on my hood. As I picked up my pace on Whiskey Bottom Road it began to snow. The temperature was so cold, the snow was dry, and it swirled around me without sticking to anything.

Pedro had been missing for three days. Was he somewhere out in this frigid weather?

I pushed on, walking as fast as I could to keep warm, hands buried deep in my pockets. I made the turn onto 198 and broke into a jog. It wasn't slippery yet, but the snow was thick and when the wind blew, the powder on the ground whirled up around my face, making it hard to see.

When I finally reached Burrito Burro, the snow was sticking and turning everything white. Cars were starting to slide and fishtail on 198. I pushed through the glass doors and stamped my feet on the rubber mat inside, grateful for the sudden warmth.

The enticing smell of chili made me decide to order something as soon as I got my ID card. There were several people in line at the counter, but I caught the eye of the gal I'd talked to before, pointed in the direction of Bic's office, and mouthed, "Is Bic back there?"

"He's all yours," she said, her eyes cold, her mouth downturned with contempt for me. A sudden rush of empathy for illegals like the Pedrozas swept through me. Feeling isolated and unwanted was a terrible thing.

I walked down the hall, rapped on Bic's door, and when I heard him tell me to come in, I stepped inside. A blonde woman in an expensive looking black coat sat in one of the chairs facing Bic's desk. With her back to me, I couldn't see her face, but there was something about her that seemed familiar.

"Nikki," Bic said, almost cheerfully. "If you've got the cash, I've got your Social Security card. Have a seat while I get it."

I didn't really want to sit down and it seemed odd that the woman didn't even turn her head to look at me. As I stepped closer, Bic came out from behind his desk.

"I'll be right back," he said, walking past me as I lowered myself into the office chair.

The woman finally turned her head to look at me. I recognized her immediately as the woman in the paddock the day Silver Punch was claimed by Ravinsky.

Dr. Vivian Braygler had been the only person in the paddock who'd shown no emotional attachment to the horse, and I understood why. I was looking into eyes as cold and uncaring as the snow outside.

Hands suddenly grabbed my upper arms.

"Get off me!" I yelled. "Stop it!"

"Hold her still," Vivian said. She opened her shiny black purse and withdrew a hypodermic needle and a syringe.

"Let go of me, you weird fuck!" I shouted.

Bic twisted my arm up behind my back until I shrieked with pain. He clamped his other hand over my mouth, stifling my scream for help before it left my mouth. He was a much heavier and stronger than me. It was like fighting a bear.

Vivian grabbed the bottom of my coat. She pulled the hem up, then shoved the needle of her syringe through the denim of my jeans and into my thigh. I fought and kicked, struggling against the dizzy grayness that swept through and over me. I lost my ability to see, and became disoriented. For a moment I was certain they'd buried me in a drift of soft, white snow.

I could hear, but was unable to see, move, or speak. It felt like I was being carried. I heard Bic's voice, and sensed bitter cold for a moment. Then there was nothing, nothing at all.

12

I was lying on my cot, except I couldn't smell the horses, or the lingering traces of liniment and molasses. The air around me smelled foreign, almost medicinal. Was I in a hospital?

I opened my eyes and saw a white ceiling and florescent lighting above me. I tried to sit up, but something stopped me. Turning my head to one side, I saw a strap holding my arm down. Something else bound my legs.

What had happened to me? Turning my head to the other side, I saw a hospital gurney next to me. A boy lay there with his eyes closed. He had cherub lips that prickled a memory. Where had I seen them before?

I tried to raise up, but was defeated by the straps. I lifted my head as high as I could, but a wave of dizziness forced me to close my eyes.

Breathe, Nikki. Move slow.

The dizziness cleared and I tried again, only more carefully. I stared at the boy. A silver medallion on his neck winked at me as it reflected the florescent light.

Recognition rushed me. *Pedro!* He lay so still, but I could see his chest rising and falling. He must to be drugged. Like me.

Beyond him, another gurney. Again, I strained my neck up as much as I could. A dark-haired girl was laying there, apparently another victim of drugs. I had to drop my head as more dizziness flooded through me.

But where in God's name were we? What was this place?

Memory hit me like a sledgehammer. The Brayglers. Bic and Vivian. They had done this. They'd made us prisoners.

I lay there with my eyes closed. What was Dr. Braygler doing? Images from TV shows like "Law & Order: Special Victims Unit" raced through my head. Were we going to be sold as slaves? Or used as plastic surgery guinea pigs?

Fear gripped me, releasing a shot of adrenalin. I struggled harder to sit up. The straps on my arms were not that tight. I wiggled one arm, drawing it up until my wrist was about to slide free of the strap. I heard a door shut, voices and footsteps.

I slid my arm back, closed my eyes, and slowed my breathing, pretending I was still knocked out. The footsteps stopped, and the voices became a quiet murmur. I turned my head to look in the opposite direction from Pedro. There was a door. The voices were on the other side. The words too low for me to understand.

I glanced at Pedro. He was still out, and so was the girl. But why was I awake? Had they given me a different drug? Then I remembered.

Mom had had trouble with sedatives. The doctors had told her she was a fast metabolizer, that her body processed some drugs so fast that . . . What was it she'd told me? Something about the drugs not reaching optimal blood levels. She's said it was genetic and that I might need higher than normal doses, just like her.

I heard the knob turn and a click as the lock on the other side released. They were coming. I lay perfectly still with my eyes closed, working to breathe slowly and evenly.

"Man, you really knocked them out, Aunt Viv."

It was Bic talking. And then I heard the voice that had ordered him to hold me still as she'd shut my world down. *Vivian.*

"The new girl will be out for a long time," she said. "The other two will need a shot in a couple of hours. Help me change their ringers."

"What about Nikki? Aren't you gonna stick an IV in her, too?"

"She won't be here long enough to need one. If I get the second phone call, we'll be doing the surgeries tonight. You're ready to make the run, right?"

"I *told* you I was, Aunt Viv."

It took more will than I'd known I possessed to lie still. *Surgeries?* I clamped down on my terror. If Vivian knew I was awake, she'd put me to sleep forever.

"So what are you gonna take?" His voice seemed to hold a sick eagerness.

"I'll know for sure when the call comes. Certainly all three hearts. And probably the kidneys.

"And Uncle Bob is going to serve up what's left to his pigs, right?"

"You already know that, Bic. I find your interest in the details to be unattractively ghoulish."

"*Me*? I'm not the one cutting their hearts out."

"That's enough! Hand me that ringer. Let's get this done. I've got a lot to do before tonight."

After that it was quiet except for the sound of Vivian doing something with the plastic bags I'd seen attached to poles that stood by the two gurneys. Pedro and been hooked up for three days, and who knew how long the poor girl had been here.

"You'll be at Burrito all afternoon, right?" Vivian asked.

"I already *told* you I got deliveries coming in. Where else would I be?"

"Fine. You just make sure you get over here the minute I call you. The time between harvesting the organs and getting them to the hospital in New York is very limited."

"So," Bic said, "if we get the three hearts and six kidneys, how much do I make?"

"You'll get your share. Come on, we're done here."

I heard their footsteps, then the door closed, and I heard the lock click. Their steps receded, and the only sound in the room was the soft breathing of my drugged roommates.

Frantically, I wriggled my arm again until I got my wrist and hand free of the strap. Raising up on my free elbow, I scanned the room. It was maybe ten by twelve feet. Beyond the girl, against the far wall, there were cabinets above a counter top that had drawers underneath. Next to that was a stack of red waste cartons labeled "biological hazard." The sight of them made me sick with fear.

Using my free hand, I unstrapped my other arm and went to work on my legs. The restraints must have been used to keep me from rolling off the gurney. Apparently Vivian was confident she didn't need to lock us down, that her drugs would take care of that.

If I hadn't inherited Mom's genes, I'd be dead. Fortunately, I had, and I was off that gurney in seconds.

After hurrying to Pedro's side, I touched his face and felt his wrist for a pulse. I didn't really know how to read a pulse, but to me, it felt steady and strong. There was no time to check the girl. I had to get *out!*

I ran to the door. Of course, it was locked. But a Baltimore schoolmate of questionable character had bragged to me once that if the lock was located in the door knob, he could simply knock the handle off the door and then open it. I remembered what he'd said.

"Just kick the sucker off with your foot."

I wasn't sure I could do that, and darted to the cabinets to look for something I could use, like a hammer. The first cabinet was filled with bandages, boxes of surgical thread, and packages containing rolls of gauze. I pulled open one of the drawers. It was like an expensive kitchen drawer with numerous sections for silverware, except instead of knives and forks there were scalpels.

Seeing them, my knees sagged and I had to steady myself against the counter top.

Find something to use, Nikki. Get out of here!

I opened another cabinet to find a collection of electric saws. One was solid metal and shaped like a big hair dryer, except where the blower would be there was a blade. I grabbed the handle, rushed to the door, and pressed my ear against it. Nothing. If Vivian or Bic were nearby, I couldn't hear them.

Using the heavy casing around the saw's electric motor, I smashed the door handle, terrified someone would hear the noise. It took three tries before the knob fell off, and the impact hurt my hand and ran up my arm to my shoulder. I didn't care. If I couldn't get out, I'd be dead.

Staring at the opening I'd made in the door, I found the spindle was still inside. I pushed it through with my fingers and it fell to the floor on the opposite side, taking the other knob with it. I stared into the hole. A horizontal bolt remained. It connected to the latch still holding the door shut. I grasped the metal with a finger and thumb and pulled it back. The door opened.

I leaned out and listened. Nothing. Before me was a long hallway. At the far end a lighted sign indicated an exit. I ran down the hall past what I thought were examining rooms on either side. A nurse emerged from one of them as I streaked by.

"Can I help you?"

"No. I was just leaving."

"Did you have an appointment?"

I kept running, finally reaching the door at the end of the hall. Any sense of caution was gone. Bursting through it, I found myself in a waiting room with soft lighting and swanky looking furniture. Women were reading magazines and fiddling with smart phones and iPads. A receptionist called out to me, and the nurse from the hallway started to chase me as I crashed through the waiting room, swung the exit door open, and fled into the main lobby. I erupted through the glass exit doors and ran from the building, heading toward 198.

It may have stopped snowing, but running was still treacherous. My feet slid out from under me and I went down hard onto the snow-covered sidewalk. Rolling to my hands and knees, I stood.

The sound of pounding feet made me whirl. Bic! He'd come from the lobby, was running after me, and closing ground fast.

13

I stared at the angry red splotches on his otherwise bloodless cheeks as he ran toward me. He got so close, he stretched his hands out to grab me.

I took off again, and behind me I heard him fall and curse. Seeing a gas station with a food mart, I ran past the pumps and darted inside. Ducking low so Bic wouldn't be able to see me in the minimart's aisles, I zipped through a couple of them and out the door on the far side.

Just ahead, a guy of about twenty was climbing into his car next to a gas pump. I yanked open the passengers' door and plunged inside.

"You have to help me! Please!" I pointed to where Bic had already come through the door of the minimart and was running toward us. "He's trying to hurt me! Please. Get out of here!"

He took one look at Bic and said, "Shit!"

He cranked his engine and we fishtailed out of the gas station and pulled onto 198. He drove about two blocks, turned into a lot outside a Laundromat, and stopped his car.

"What the hell was that about," he asked. He had scruffy hair, and a beard, but his steady eyes reassured me.

"I have to call the police. There's a guy and a girl in trouble. They need help!"

"What are you, a drama queen?" Glancing at my expression, he said, "Forget I asked. Here." In his hand was a cell phone.

I called 911 and a dispatcher came on the line. I tried to explain what had happened. The guy next to me shook his head like he'd never heard anything so farfetched in his life.

The dispatcher wanted my name. I couldn't tell her, the police were looking for me.

"Nikki Bernstein." I said, somehow coming up with the name of the Pimlico guy who'd split his bet with me.

I made it through the call with the dispatcher without tripping any landmines, but at some point, I'd have to come up with an explanation for my connection to Bic. I could hardly say I'd been buying false ID.

The dispatcher kept me on the phone while we waited for a police cruiser to show up. Glancing at the clock on the dash, I was surprised to see it was just past three. I hadn't been knocked out for long, but that it had happened at all left me shaken.

When a squad car pulled up next to us, I was glad to see two fully armed Anne Arundel County officers climb out, at least until they started questioning me.

My rescuer, who said his name was Mike, listened to the story I told the cops like it was the greatest entertainment he'd had all year.

"Yeah," he said, when they asked him, "this crazy looking guy was chasing her. Creeped me out, man."

When I realized they had called an ambulance for me, I got mad.

"I don't need a stupid ambulance. I want to go back to the clinic! Have the police even gone there yet?"

One cop, whose muscular body and unrelenting manner reminded me of a bull dog, said, "Miss, you need to calm down and be seen by an EMT. Officers are handling the situation at the clinic. It's not your problem."

When the ambulance arrived, the cop turned me over to the EMTs, and Mike watched as they shepherded me inside the ambulance.

"Hey, Nikki," he called, "good luck, okay?"

I nodded.

"Bernstein, right?" he asked.

"Yeah, Nikki Bernstein." I was such a liar.

What seemed like hours later, I was still in the emergency section of Laurel Hospital, sitting on a gurney in one of those little curtained cubicles. They'd taken my clothes and made me wear a hospital gown that was impossible to fasten.

A nurse had checked my vital signs to see if I'd retained any adverse effect from the drug Braygler had given me. Apparently I didn't, but she'd still drawn blood for a toxicology report. Apparently the doctor I'd seen earlier had ordered the test.

But no one had answered my questions about Pedro or the girl.

The curtain drew back as the doctor reappeared. He had light brown skin, smooth black hair and badge that said Dr. Basu.

"Miss Bernstein," he said, "we'll have to wait on the toxicology report, but you seem to have come through this quite well."

"Can I go?"

"Do you have a parent or guardian who can take you home?"

"Sure," I said. "They'll be here soon."

"That's good, because you can't be discharged until someone arrives to take you."

I planned to bolt the minute he left. A nurse had already asked me about insurance and payment. I'd lied and said my parents would take care of it.

"But please," I said to Doctor Basu, "can you tell me about the other kids that were with me in that plastic surgery clinic?" By now the lack of answers had frustrated me to the point that my voice was rising with anger. "I really need to hear that they are all right! They *must* here in this hospital."

He rubbed his eyes, and thought a moment. "Oh, yes. I did find out for you."

Had he ever planned on telling me?

"The attending doctor thinks they should be fine. They have woken up and appear to be physically unharmed. I can't speak to their emotional state."

"Can I see the boy, Pedro?"

"No, I'm sorry. Only immediate family. His mother and father are with him."

Well, at least there was that. "What about the people that abducted us?"

"I'm sorry. I don't know anything about that." His lips thinned into a tight line as his stare became more penetrating. "Did your parents say when they'd be here?"

I didn't like the growing skepticism in his eyes. "Um, they just left word with the nurse that they'd be here soon." I faked a smile.

I exhaled with relief when as Basu left the cubicle. Seconds later, I stuck my head out to see him retreating down the hall in the distance. I found my clothes in a bag under the gurney. I pulled them out, got dressed, and stepped into the hall. The place was like a rabbit warren with long corridors going in all directions and I wasn't sure I could find my way out. But I had to.

If they discovered I had no identity, no money, and no family, they'd call the police or county social services for sure. Damn everything. I took a deep breath and headed in the opposite direction from where Doctor Basu had gone.

By the time I got around the first corner and saw an exit sign in the distance, I'd started crying. I tried to stop the tears, but seemed to have lost my inner strength. I felt weak, alone, and afraid.

The door beneath the red exit sign swung open and a man came through. He was tall, but stooped as if old.

Ravinsky. Was he here to see the Pedrozas? Was it possible he'd come for me?

I swiped at my tears and walked slowly toward him, feeling I was about to reach a crossroads.

When we were a few feet apart, he looked at the tears still streaming down my face.

"Oh, for God's sake," he said. "I can't have my stable help crying all the time."

The words "my stable help" were as sweet as anything I'd ever heard. I sniffed, and wiped the back of my hand across my nose. "Have you seen Maria or Pedro?"

"Yes. They're fine. They'll be at the barn later." He glanced at my hands which had started shaking. "Listen to me. The Brayglers are in police custody. They can't hurt you, okay?"

"She was going to *kill* us."

"I know," he said, shaking his head as if he still couldn't get his mind around it. He put a hand on my shoulder and gently pushed me toward the exit door.

"Come on Nikki, let's go home."

49150378R10053

Made in the USA
Middletown, DE
06 October 2017